# BLOOD OF THE LAMB . . .

"Stop right there, mister, or I'll shoot you."

The kid was going to kill him, the Penetrator realized. The tiny, nail-bitten finger tightened to whiteness on the trigger of the diminutive Czech Model 61, 7.65 submachine gun. Mark forced down his revulsion and reluctance at harming a mere child and fired a three-round burst from the Sidewinder.

The trio of big .45 slugs tore into the short, skinny little boy's legs. He screamed and fell. His two companions, filled with the horror of their first-hand introduction to violence, dropped their fire-arms and fled.

Quickly the Penetrator climbed over the fence and hurried toward his car. He climbed behind the wheel of the Aspen and sped off into the darkness.

The boys' ranch had been in a higher state of readiness than the previous institutions he'd visited. There hadn't been any Korean guards around. Some of the more advanced juvenile assassins apparently handled those duties.

And, oh, God, he'd killed one kid.

Sick from the enormous burden this hopeless mission had placed upon him, the Penetrator drove on toward Provo and another raid on an SIE school for kiddie killers. . . .

# THE PENETRATOR SERIES:

No. 47

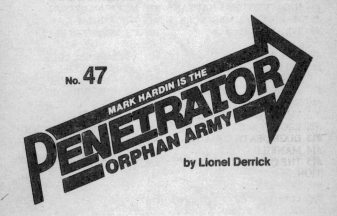

MARK HARDIN IS THE
PENETRATOR
ORPHAN ARMY

by Lionel Derrick

PINNACLE BOOKS         NEW YORK

Penetrator .47: Orphan Army

An original Pinnacle Books edition, published for
the first time anywhere.

First printing, September 1982

ISBN: 0-523-41554-0

Cover illustration by George Wilson

*Printed in the United States of America*

PINNACLE BOOKS, INC.
1430 Broadway
New York, New York 10018

*This one is for*
*John F. Lowe,*
*Scholar, Historian and Friend*

# ORPHAN ARMY

# 1

## DEATH OF A TITAN

Only a scattered handful of lights illuminated the upper-story windows of the concrete and steel cavern on Madison Avenue. On the street level, color TV monitors that faced the large display windows of the CCN main office flickered out at a sparse flow of indifferent pedestrians. The hour-long, eleven o'clock nightly news broadcast was coming to an end.

Near the top of the towering skyscraper, one glow emanated from the office of Walter Cottler, world-renowned, Pulitzer-Prize-winning editorial commentator. Cottler sat at an electronic type-writer; his face—familiar to millions of Americans for over thirty years—wore a grim expression. His fingers flew in sporadic movements across the keyboard and letters appeared, to spell out spidery black words on the off-white newsprint rolled into the machine. Cottler paused, then typed again. Then stopped to read his lead paragraph.

"There is a large organization existing in the world today that is little known to the average American, yet its headquarters is located in Felder Square here in New York City," he read aloud from the copy in the typewriter. "Its members come from several European nations, Canada, the United States, and the Orient. It is called the *Société Internationale d'Élite*. As its name implies, it is an organization of elitists.

"The membership consists of One Worlders, dedicated to establishing an economic and political stranglehold on the peoples of all nations, using a conglomerate of industrial and business giants that will constitute one single governmental unit, answerable only to its international Board of Directors. Its rule will be absolute and will ultimately replace every form of national sovereignty known today.

"If this sounds like the plot for *Star Wars Three*, or the ravings of the Radical Right, believe me, it most assuredly is not. The SIE exists, and, far more important and dangerous than its origins and history—which we will cover in later segments of this special report—is the disturbing news of the SIE's most recent activities." Walter Cottler licked dry lips and then resumed typing.

That bungling old fool of a night watchman had nearly caught them. Not from carelessness or from tripping an alarm, but by accident. Chion Bok looked at his partner, Qwan Ti Ree. The young, highly skilled agent of the *Kung Hop Chee*, the National Security Service, winked and nodded reassurance. The elderly security guard, his throat cut from side to side, lay in a spreading pool of his blood in the ground-floor fire stairwell. Two minutes had passed since Qwan Ti had killed him, and no one had come looking for him.

"It is time to climb," Chion suggested.

"Yes. We must hurry with our mission."

Walter Cottler completed the last line of a paragraph and took the sheet of newsprint from the machine. He inserted a fresh piece of twenty-pound bond in the IBM Electronic 175 and punched the play key. The electronic-chip, ten-page memory began to reproduce his script from the first line of page one.

From time to time, Cottler stopped the machine, deleted a word, added another, then let the ball speed across the white field, leaving behind the tracks of his thoughts. When the last line went on at a half page, he returned to the original copy mode and started to type, speaking aloud as he did.

"Information has reached CCN News Central of a series of meetings recently held between ranking leaders of the SIE and representatives of the North . . . "

Cottler stopped reading at the sound of a slight noise near the door at his back. He turned in his massive swivel chair in time to see two short, stocky Orientals rushing at him.

"Wha-a-a . . . "

Thin slivers of steel glinted in their hands a brief second in the light from the work lamp. Then the intruders plunged their knives into Walter Cottler's chest and abdomen.

The famous newscaster tried to scream at the incredible agony that swarmed outward from his wounds. No sound came. Oily sweat burst on his forehead and his vision wavered. He discovered that by enormous effort he could move the fingers and hand of one arm. Slowly, carefully, he inched toward a small switch concealed in the legwell of his desk. At last a nearly inaudible click informed him of success. He had the words formed in his mind, wanted to shout them out for the hidden recorder, but only a breathy whisper issued from his blood-stained lips. Movement near him attracted his attention.

Cottler watched helplessly while his two assassins hurriedly rummaged through the items on his work desk. One grabbed up the pages of his manuscript and stuffed them inside a loose Windbreaker. His companion similarly disposed of Cottler's notes propped on his copy stand. The two men turned away and began to sort through stacks of film cans and videotape boxes on a floor-to-ceiling rack nearby. Cottler felt a benumbing sense of frustrated helplessness when he again tried to raise his hand.

Nothing.

All sensation had fled from his body. Behind him he heard discarded reels, film footage not of interest to the intruders, strike the floor. With a supreme effort, he managed to turn his head for another glimpse of his murderers. Then Walter Cottler's vision blurred further, light and darkness merged into a skyrocket display of bright pinpoints. Dimly he heard receding footsteps, the door to his office close, then his hearing diminished to soundlessness.

Cottler tried to gasp, choked on a fountain of his own blood, and died.

# 2

## APPEAL FROM ABOVE

Black banner headlines and film clips with long, sonorously narrated voice-over eulogies informed the world of the murder of the Dean of American News Broadcasters. Walter Cottler was gone but definitely not forgotten, even by competitors. Only one man, apparently, remained ignorant of the assassination.

Mark Hardin had not seen a newspaper or television set in four days. What's more, he didn't miss them. Mark sat in a low, folding beach chair on the Arizona bank of the Colorado River. He held a big Shakespear rod in his hands, equipped with a sturdy surf-casting reel with powerful star drag, and hoped fervently that this time he might snag one of those thirty-five- or forty-pound channel cats that inhabited these waters. So far his luck hadn't been all that good, though the freezer compartment in the Brown Beast's camper held an ample collection of bass fillets and he'd breakfasted each morning on smaller catfish. Barefoot, his shirt open to reveal his sun-bronzed chest, Mark leaned back with a contented sigh and took a sip from a large glass of iced tea. With sundown only half an hour away, the big ones should begin to stir and feed before long. That's when he'd get the bites.

Suddenly the pencillike device in his shirt pocket began to insistently beep at him. Someone was trying to reach him on the radio phone. He shook his head regretfully, put his pole in the holder, and rose. In two swift strides he reached the truck.

"You're a hard guy to find," came a familiar voice over the line. "It took me half an hour to run down your location."

"Hello, Dan. So what world-shaking events cause you to disturb my peaceful fishing?"

"Hey, Arrowsmith, don't growl like that. Have you read today's paper? Seen the news on TV?"

"No. And I don't intend to. This is a vacation, guy."

"Well, get a local rag, read it, and call me back. I'll be in my office until midnight our time."

"What's it all about, Dan?"

"Read first, then we'll talk. Bye."

Dan Griggs, who headed a Justice Department special task force on white-collar and organized crime, had his office in an obscure corner of the fourth-floor corridor of a building on Seventeenth Street Northwest, across from the old Treasury Building, in Washington, D.C. Mark Hardin didn't work for Dan and he didn't particularly like his fishing expedition being interrupted. He also knew that Dan would never hunt him down like he had unless something definitely big had happened.

Mark reeled in, stowed his gear in the camper, and climbed into the cab of the onetime 1977 Ford three-quarter ton pickup. He fired up the much-altered engine and drove toward the distant neon lights of Lake Havasu City. On the way he passed by London Bridge, looking displaced and anachronous where it spanned a portion of a man-made lake instead of the Thames.

At the foot of its sprawling Arizona-side pylon sprawled the pseudo-English village creaed by millionaire manufacturer Robert McCulloch, the chain-saw magnate. Despite the obvious artificiality of Soho-on-the-desert, it managed to create an aura of charm peculiar to only a few of the most successful, so-called theme parks. Mark entered the outskirts of the small city on the Colorado and stopped at a liquor store.

Immediately his eyes widened at sight of the headline on the *Phoenix Sun.* Beside it, a copy of the *San Diego Union* blared the same news. WALTER COTTLER MURDERED!

The boldface type left no doubt in Mark's mind about the purpose behind Dan's call. He purchased both editions, got a six-pack of Henry Weinhardt's, and returned to his campsite. There he spread out the two newspapers and read the stories by the light of a Coleman lantern. He'd do a little night fishing with the gasoline lamp after he called Dan—provided he had the time.

"Dan," Mark said quickly when the Justice Department man came on the line. "I've got the basics now. At least what the papers said. Cottler was murdered in his office. Also a night watchman died in the lobby, right? And whoever did it rifled the files and stole some film. Anything more I should know?"

"Some. That's the official version released to the press early this morning. For obvious reasons, certain things were left out. For instance: In his dying moments, Cottler recovered long enough to activate a concealed recorder. You can clearly hear the assailants trashing Cottler's office. Some film cans rattle and then they leave. Cottler's voice comes on for a second or a bit more. He's whispering. Over and over, he says, 'The orphanage, the orphanage.' "

"What else, Dan?"

"His manuscript and all the notes for his current project, a special report in seven parts, are missing. The assassins made one mistake, though. Cottler was using an IBM Electronic 175. NYPD detectives were able to play back the first nine and a half pages of the manuscript from chip memory. Cottler ended with the word *North.* We have to assume he was interrupted at that point and murdered. Here's what he had so far." Dan quickly read the text of Walter Cottler's first segment on the SIE.

"Hummm," came Mark's reply when Dan finished. "The SIE. So they're back and apparently more than willing to murder to prevent anyone knowing too much about them."

"That's why I thought you'd be interested. Are you?"

"Damn right I am. If anyone's number-one man on their hit parade, it has to be me. Any idea if Cottler had a line on what went down in D.C. a few years back?"

"Not with all his research gone. You want to do this one for me?"

"No, Dan. On my own, as always. I'll keep you posted though and may ask for some assistance occasionally, but nothing more."

"Look, Arrowsmith, you might be one damn fine one-man army, but this is big. I'd guess it to be hairier than the Mafia."

"Nothing, my friend, is that big. Let me handle it and I'll give you what I dig out. So long."

Well, that blew the fishing all to hell, but ignoring the SIE could get him dead in a hurry, Mark knew. He packed and started the long drive back to California and the Stronghold.

The Stronghold, a fantastic underground mansion built inside a borax mine in the Calico Mountains outside Barstow, California, in the Mojave Desert by retired geology professor Willard Haskins, served as headquarters for the man known to millions around the world only as the Penetrator.

Mark Hardin was the Penetrator, that well-kept secret known to less than a dozen persons. It had not been Mark's intention to make a career of crime fighting or world saving. He had enjoyed a slightly higher than average acedemic performance at UCLA and an outstanding record as an athlete. Vietnam had come along and Mark had enlisted. He declined an offer to attend officer training and steadily rose in the ranks to sergeant first class. His military specialty was intelligence, and Mark got combat experience in a dozen battles and in probes behind the enemy's lines, twice going far into North Vietnam to terminate high-ranking Communist officers and important civilians. Then he returned to the states and counterintelligence school.

Mark's second tour in 'Nam resulted in the discovery of a large blackmarket ring, operating in

Saigon, that involved many American military personnel, including one brigadier general. He did his work thoroughly and made a report. When no arrests followed his revelation, Mark became disenchanted with the regime in command in Saigon. He took his story to the AP wire service editor in that city. Within days the world knew and Mark became the subject of a reprimand. The army began taking the guilty into custody and Mark felt he could accept his chewing out in stride. He didn't count on the vindictiveness of the few who escaped punishment.

A few days following the mass roundup of blackmarket members, those who had avoided the dragnet lured Mark to an abandoned warehouse on the waterfront and there severely beat him. Broken bones and internal injuries nearly finished the job they thought had been completed. Mark was sent to Okinawa and then on to Letterman General in San Francisco. Slowly his body healed, but his spirit remained low and a discharge for medical reasons didn't help diminish his bitterness.

It took the well-meaning efforts of Mark's former football coach from UCLA to get him on the road to normalcy once again. At his suggestion, Mark journeyed to Barstow and out to the Calico Mountains to meet Professor Haskins. They formed an immediate liking for each other and Mark agreed to stay in the spacious underground mansion, the Stronghold. Later a wandering Cheyenne medicine chief, David Red Eagle, came into Mark's life and undertook a regimen of physical and mental conditioning that rapidly restored Mark's health and superb physique. Events that followed brought Donna Morgan, the professor's niece, into Mark's world. Romance bloomed and all went well until the Mafia decided to take a hand.

Donna Morgan died and Mark went on to exact bloody vengeance from the Cosa Nostra family of Don Pietro Scarelli.

Out of this conflict the Penetrator was born.

Even then, Mark didn't see himself as a vengeful Robin Hood, or a self-appointed executioner for those who escaped the retribution of police and courts. After forty-six missions, though, all thought of doing anything else had left him long ago. He did what he did because he was the best there was at doing it. The parasites always cropped up and the Penetrator struck hard and fast to exterminate them. Mark Hardin was well equipped to carry out his role.

Mark was a powerfully built man, a pair of inches over six feet, with dark black hair and eyes and a thin line of mustache to match. His teeth, white and even in a darkly bronzed, square-jawed face, were rarely seen, for he smiled infrequently. He maintained his body weight at a hefty two hundred five pounds without any effort at dieting and moved with the smooth, graceful fluidity of a jungle cat. His features, somber and noble as a George Catlin portrait of a Cheyenne chief, took on a deadly aura when he frowned.

He had that natural athlete's quality about him that caused men to admire and respect him on sight and women to grow weak kneed. He had mastered the martial arts of karate and firearms and, under Red Eagle's tutelage, learned the Native American fighting style of Orenda Keowa, as well as the spiritual and physical skills of the Cheyenne Dog Soldier lodge. His carefully tuned senses made him an ideal fighting machine.

While Mark drove across the vast emptiness of the California desert, northwestward toward Barstow, he realized that he would need every bit of that skill if he were to enter another battle against the *Société Internationale d'Élite*.

David Felder sat behind the broad, polished expanse of his desk at the Grace Bank in Manhattan. Only a small blotter and a pen caddy broke the empty perfection of the huge slab of Brazilian ironwood. In his hand he held a large file, flipping from page to page. After a few silent moments, he stopped and looked at his visitor. He ran well-manicured fingers through the gray hair at one temple, patted his lush, full head of hair into militarily precise alignment, and frowned.

"Dammit, I told you we should have used our own men. Those slopes bungled the job. They were supposed to make Cottler disappear, create some confusion for a few days. If our North Korean comrades can't provide more competent agents than that, what the hell are we wasting time on the training schools for?"

Brian DeGraff studied his superior in SIE for a moment. His pale, ice blue eyes took in Felder's eight-hundred-dollar hand-tailored suit, white silk shirt, narrow tie, and the broad, confident set of shoulders. He stroked his long jawline with pale, spatulate fingers and wet his thick, full lips before replying. "Take it easy, Mr. Felder.

"Look, we have the situation in hand. Okay, so that memory typewriter of Cottler's retained some of his information on the organization. So what?

Nobody else is going to carry on. Not with the film gone. You know these press people. They'll piss and moan about one of theirs being murdered for a few days and beat the drum about their precious First Amendment rights for a few days and then some other big story will come along and it will all be forgotten."

"I'm afraid I don't share your cynicism on this matter, Brian. This isn't some pip-squeak cameraman getting shot down by the Jamestown freaks. Cottler was—*Cottler,* a damned institution in this country. Hell, the queen of England has already sent condolences to CCN. And even I have to attend the memorial service tomorrow. The Feds are in on it because Cottler received threats from some organized-crime people not long ago."

"The Feds?"

"Exactly. Some special task force on organized crime, headed by a guy named Griggs. We have to be extremely careful."

"What about the other matter you wanted to talk over?"

Felder gestured with the file in his hand. "The Penetrator. I have the file on him right here. You weren't one of us when he struck at our cell in Washington, D.C., were you? Let me tell you, he tore apart an apparatus that had taken years to put into place. There weren't any amateurs among them and yet this—this *Penetrator,*" Felder spoke the name as though his mouth had suddenly been filled with manure, "came on like an entire combat force and literally burned down our headquarters around the ears of our best fighting men.

"I'll swear to God that he's the one that wiped

out the weather generator in space. He sat right here in this office, disguised as a Latino, a Panamanian business man, and conned us into revealing the bank's involvement with the Third World space center."

"I've heard of him, of course, but why do you think he might get involved with this current project?"

"Use your head, Brian. When the man, whoever he really is, learns that there is even a fringe possibility of SIE involvement in Cottler's death, he'll come after us. He has every reason to do so. It seems the Washington group killed a friend of his. That was all it took then. He didn't let up until the entire program to take control of the government was exposed, along with the identity of everyone involved, and he managed to decimate our ranks in a bloodbath.

"Apparently all one has to do is get the Penetrator excited about something and—events simply happen. Destructively so, I might add."

"He's only one man, Mr. Felder."

"True. Even so, I want the directors at every institution alerted and a description of the Penetrator circulated to them. If even the remotest possibility exists that this bastard might get on to our plans, I want him stopped—cold."

"Terminated?"

"Yes, Brian. Terminated."

# 3

# ROTTEN CORE IN THE BIG APPLE

AMTRAK. What a great way to travel—provided one had the time.

The Penetrator figured he had three days to spare. He wanted the extra hours to sort out the information provided by Dan Griggs and his own computer banks. He had flown his Mooney 201 partway across the country to Albuquerque, New Mexico, arriving there late afternoon on the day after Griggs had contacted him about Cottler's death. In Albuquerque he had gone to S & S Arms to pick up a new, full-barrel silencer model High Standard Trophy Sid McQueen had built for him and a reconditioned MAC silencer for his Sidewinder. McQueen knew Mark Hardin as Jason Talbot, a New Mexico resident, licensed to own automatic weapons and suppressors.

Early the next morning, the Penetrator left the bustling desert city aboard Santa Fe's Super Chief, AMTRAK passenger run to Chicago. He would make a transfer there to the crack train once named the Twentieth Century Limited. Mark loved train travel, when his schedule permitted. His romance with the rails went back to childhood, when he maintained model railroad lay-outs whenever he could.

The clacking wheels, rhythmic sway of the coaches, and genteel charm of dining-car service appealed to his sense of what true luxury was all about. A few miles out of Albuquerque, the porter brought a small fold-out table to Mark's roomette and the Penetrator placed the Cottler documents on it. He leaned back in the spacious comfort of his upholstered seat and reflected a moment on his brief conversation with David Red Eagle before he had departed from the Stronghold. They discussed a problem that had been much on Mark's mind of late. Despite disagreement, he felt the ancient Cheyenne medicine chief would follow his suggestions no matter how reluctantly.

"I realize the Beast has a good many miles left, David," the Penetrator had told his physical-training instructor the previous night. The rust brown Ford pickup had been their mainstay of ground transportation for several years. Modified out of any semblance to factory original, it had served them well. "But consider this. We've used that pickup a lot. Everyone around Barstow is getting to know it, not to mention a few elements of the Mafia and any stragglers from the Aryan Brotherhood who might have escaped Coalville. Then there's the maintenance factor. Old vehicles take more care. It's time to look into a new truck."

"Don't forget that the Beast was modified for four-wheel operation," Red Eagle reminded Mark, a drawn-out look of sadness on his face.

"So? We can get another four-by-four, stock,

from the factory without modification. With the use of strip paint it gives us an unlimited number of 'different'-looking trucks."

"True. Yet, the Brown Beast has always met our needs."

Mark placed a friendly, consoling hand on Red Eagle's shoulder. He understood the old Cheyenne's reluctance. "Let's face it, my friend," he chided gently, "you're getting too conservative in your old age. I'm not advocating change for change's sake. What I had in mind, actually, was two vehicles. A good pickup for you and some sort of four-wheel drive, high-center rig for off-road work for me—something that we could armor."

The idea of a protected auto for his protégé excited Red Eagle. "Such as?"

"I've been thinking about several. The Ford Bronco is nice. Also the Dodge RAM Charger."

"What about the Blazer?"

"It's the third one I've considered. As to the pickup, I have a little surprise for you. I wanted something that stands out so much that it becomes inconspicuous when taking into consideration the uses we'll be putting it to."

"You mean along the lines of the old espionage adage that the best place to hide something is right out in the open?"

"Exactly. And for that, there's only one choice—the Dodge D-50. It's a sporty little thing, carries a large load, and is racy enough to be overlooked by anyone hunting our operation."

Red Eagle frowned. Sporty? Racy? How would it look for a respected medicine chief of the Cheyenne Nation to be wheeling around in a truck that could be described by such words? Unthinkable. Yes . . . "Go on. I'm—intrigued."

"Later. Look, to save time, while I'm gone on this Cottler thing, I want you to check out the three off-road rigs and the D-50. Talk to the sheriff's deputies, the Border Patrol guys. If you can come up with any better candidates, I'll listen. But give every one a good going over and spare nothing. We want only the best. Then, when I get back, we can make a final decision." The conversation faded into the faint, distant wail of the diesel-locomotive horn that sounded far forward on the train, and Mark Hardin bought his attention to the slim sheaf of papers covering the murder of Walter Cottler.

Another thing he liked about travel by railroad, the Penetrator mused while he studied the first page, was that he could bring almost any sort of weapons or munitions aboard. No one hijacked passenger trains; consequently, security precautions, like those at airports, were nonexistent. He would arrive in New York with all the armament he had decided he would need on this mission.

The Penetrator's first stop in New York was an office on the ninth floor of a dingy-fronted building on West Forty-seventh Street, in the shadow of the Empire State Building. A formidable-looking receptionist of middle years greeted him and, upon hearing the cover name he had chosen to use on this mission, instructed Mark to enter Office C, on the other side of an ancient, worn wooden rail.

No one waited for the Penetrator here, only a file folder on an otherwise Spartanly bare desk.

Mark opened the manila jacket and examined the contents.

"Hummm," he mused aloud. "Justice Department credentials in the name of Greg Miller, a tape cassette, and a transcript of Cottler's manuscript." From the sparse data available, he surmised that Dan Griggs intended to play this one extremely close to the chest. All right, so he was on his own. Where to start?

A desk drawer yielded a tape recorder. Mark installed the cartridge and listened to Walter Cottler's last gasped words. Then he read the seven pages of copy. A frown formed almost at once and deepened.

*The damned SIE!*

Mark thought back to that cold December day when the president's press secretary, Fred Walters, a longtime friend of Mark Hardin's and former bureau chief for the AP wire service in Saigon, had been assassinated. That had been the Penetrator's first introduction to the *Société Internationale d'Élite.* Before he had finished with them, the members of the One Worlder cabal—who masqueraded in every political guise, from the ultraleft to the far right—had reeled under the impact of Mark's brand of bloody vengeance. He thought he had crushed the nefarious organization, only to have SIE cross his path again in Montreal.

Now the specter of their evil presence arose once more to plague him. No longer a secret society, known only to its members and a few hangers-on, the SIE had "gone public." Over the past few years, the SIE had projected an image of wealth and respectability, according to the three-page summary Dan had included in the file. SIE's influence on government policy, at least until the current administration came into power, was a well-known fact. The SIE and its subsidiary organizations, the International Coalition, the INC as it was called, drew fire now from the left and the right, an effective smoke screen to mask their intentions when one considered that many of the reporters and commentators who vilified the elitist groups were themselves members. Even if the SIE had nothing directly to do with Cottler's murder, the Penetrator thought, an investigation into its activities shouldn't be overlooked. He would begin, though, with the people who had worked with Cottler, Mark decided.

"Good afternoon, Mr. Miller," a pert, smiling receptionist at the CCN building greeted the Penetrator. "Mr. Cottler's former crew persons are waiting for you, as you requested."

"Thank you, Miss, ah . . ." Mark glanced at a polished brass nameplate on the young woman's plain, functional desk. "Jennings. Where can I talk with them?"

"I've arranged a conference room for you. It's right down the hall, 2340."

"Thank you." Amazing, the amount of cooperation his Justice Department credentials had generated. Particularly from a television network whose prideful jealousy over the past few years regarding its First Amendment rights had placed it in an almost adversary relationship to the government, and DOJ in particular. It was a shame, the Penetrator reflected, that the media people failed to guard the other amendments with equal zeal. Particularly the Second Amendment. Any thinking person had to realize that without that one, the precious rights of the First Amendment, and all the others, wouldn't last long. Oh, well, the Penetrator dismissed his thoughts, ours not to reason why . . . He located Room 2340 without difficulty and opened the door.

Seven men and women sat in a variety of uncomfortable-looking Danish-modern chairs. they talked in a manner of subdued curiosity, which became instant silence the moment Mark appeared in the doorway. Seven faces turned as many sets of resigned, suspicious eyes on the Penetrator.

"Hello. I'm Greg Miller."

"We know who you are," the apparent leader of the technical crew growled acidly. "What we don't know is why we have to go over all of this again."

"Simple, really. You haven't told it to me yet." The Penetrator noticed a coffee service on a side table and walked to it. He poured himself a cup, tasted it and winced at its lukewarm bitterness.

"We don't think much of it either," a striking redhead quipped. Her words broke the tension and several of the men chuckled.

"Do they drain this out of radiators?" Mark asked.

"No," the crewcut, blond spokesman responded. "Stictly from used batteries. Okay, so we haven't told you our story. Where do we begin?"

"At the end, strangely enough." The Penetrator drew up a chair and sat in it. He had been right, it was terribly uncomfortable. "How much footage remained to be shot before Cottler's special report aired?"

Mark's competent, offhand use of professional jargon won their confidence. He could see three of those present relaxing under his bland expression and earnest, sincere voice. The moderately overwight man made the first reply.

"I suppose I'm the one to answer that." He pointed one thick, blunt index finger in the direction of the ceiling. "Walter had all the prints in his office upstairs. I'm Lyle Connors, I directed the spot and did some of the editing. We had only the final segment to complete."

"Could it be that whatever the subject of that last program happened to involve was the cause of Cottler's murder?"

"I don't see how—not any more than the previous ones."

"And the subject of the entire special report was the *Société Internationale d'Élite?*"

"Yes," Connors replied, and several of the crew nodded in agreement. "So what's that got to do with it?"

"I'm not sure," the Penetrator replied. "Can you tell me how many executives and broadcast personnel of Continental Communications Network are members of SIE?"

Several of Walter Cottler's former associates looked uncomfortable and avoided staring directly at Mark. At last the redhead spoke up.

"I'm Irene Szabo. I handled Walter's research. That was the first information he asked me to dig out."

"Say, the police didn't ask us all of this crap. Neither did the FBI," a scrawny, long-haired young man with beer-bottle-bottom glasses interrupted. "Just who are you to bring all this irrelevent stuff up?"

"I didn't get your name," the Penetrator replied calmly.

"Bob Hansen. I'm the cameraman." Hansen's prominent Adam's apple elevatored rapidly in his long, turkey-red neck.

"I am from a special DOJ task force on organized crime and white-collar criminals. The obvious fact is that someone wanted Walter Cottler dead and hired unknown persons to do the job. We have to start somewhere."

"But why with the SIE?" Hansen persisted. "Surely a prestigious international organization like that wouldn't have anything to do with murder. Even the cops weren't that stupid."

The Penetrator's scowl radiated a deadly aura that disturbed the crew members. "Don't make book on that. I've encountered the SIE before, and it's far from the paragon of virtue you seem to think it is."

"You can't be serious," Hanson blurted. The Penetrator could feel tension building in the room, hot and oppressive despite the air conditioning. Hansen went on. "Look, my dad's a member, so are a number of his friends. They're damn nice people in my book. I don't even know why Cottler wanted to do an exposé on the society."

"I won't argue the point with you, Bob," the Penetrator responded mildly. "Now that SIE has gone public, there are a lot of decent, respectable persons who have joined. Odds are, they aren't the least aware of SIE's less savory endeavors. As to Cottler's motivation, it was probably much like my own in wanting to investigate the society. The fact is, if you don't mind clichés, SIE is rotten to the core."

Bob Hansen's face flushed crimson and he surged to his feet, fists clenched, long, angular body leaning forward in a threatening posture. He thrust out his neck, chin aggressively poised, though trembling with the indignation he felt. His lips curled into a pugnacious sneer.

"I don't care if you are a Fed, Miller. There are still laws against libel and slander. You'd better watch what you say about the SIE or you'll find yourself in a lot of trouble."

"You are excused from this meeting, Mr. Hansen," the Penetrator ordered quietly.

"I'm not going. I've a right to stay here. Freedom of the press, you know."

"Get out of here, or I'll kick your ass through that door without opening it." The Penetrator's black eyes had turned onyx-hard and glittered with battle fever. He now realized that the tension he had felt and the reluctance of the other crew members to talk to him came from their knowledge that Hansen had an inside with the SIE. Apparently, some of these competent professionals in the news-gathering business had come to a similar conclusion to his own regarding the possible involvement of the SIE. If he hoped to get anything of value, he had to quickly master the situation. Mark forced his voice into a low, calm, commanding register.

"Leave the room, Bob. I won't tell you again."

Hansen's long-lobed head and shaggy hair swiveled from side to side, seeking support. He found none. He managed to overcome his anger and left the room without another word.

"Now, ah—Irene is it?—you were saying that the first thing Cottler had you check was the number of SIE members affiliated with CCN?"

"Right. And we got a bit of a surprise. The president of the conglomerate that owns CCN and three members of the board are longtime SIEs. So is the general manager of the network and two of our anchor persons, including Stan Prather, who took over Walter's place as news director. Then, of course, there's Hansen's father. He's a large stockholder, though he's not directly connected with CCN."

"I see. Did you manage to save any of the film?"

"Only a couple of negatives," Lyle Connors offered. "We made prints and the FBI took one set. We have one reel, enough material for two shows, left here. Do you want to see it?"

"I'd appreciate that."

"Th-then you seriously think the SIE is involved in Walter's murder?" Irene inquired, surprised and doubting.

"I haven't reached any conclusions at this point. I only want to cover every possibility."

Half an hour later, the Penetrator left the CCN building. On the reel of film, mostly silent, he had been able to identify several prominent persons connected with the SIE, including David Felder, president of the Grace Bank and rumored to be head of SIE's New York operation. Lyle Connors and Irene Szabo pointed out other SIE luminaries, including two U.S. senators. The latter were seen entering and leaving One Felder Square, home of not only the Grace Bank, but the Felder Foundation.

The philanthropic organization was noted for its generous endowments, including aid to private institutions, among them several orphanages. Cottler's last words on the tape, regarding orphan homes, caught in Mark's mind and he felt the persistent nudge of a curiosity bump. He'd check out that angle, he decided, the next day at the Felder Foundation.

"Good morning, Felder Foundation," a dulcet voice murmured into a thin arc of boom mike across the reception area of the eighteenth-floor charitable organization had carried to where the Penetrator sat browsing through a copy of *Business in 1990: A Look to the Future,* edited by Adam Starchild. Mark wondered how a book bearing the name of the unorthodox young financial wizard had gotten here in the haven of the Establishment and the SIE. Mark felt rested, though, and ready to take on the best the Felder people could throw at him.

On the previous afternoon, after leaving CCN, he had checked into a hotel. A good night's sleep and a hearty breakfast of corned beef hash, poached eggs, and bagels with cream cheese down the street at Manny's Deli had restored the Penetrator to fighting trim. He looked up with what he hoped to be an expectant expression when a svelte young woman approached whisperingly across the ankle-clutching, deep pile carpet. Loads of marble, rare wood, bronzes, and originals by Modigliani and Picasso provided a lush richness to the decor of the foundation's outer office. The high-fashion glamor poise of the youthful secretary in her severely cut, mannish three-piece suit enhanced the almost forbidding exclusivity of the atmosphere.

"Yes, Mr., ah, Miller. What was it you wished to see us about?"

The Penetrator rose from his chair. "Ah, you're Miss Weldon, then?"

"*Ms.* Weldon, please, if you don't mind," the impeccably turned-out junior executive replied icily.

He *did* mind, the Penetrator thought, but what the hell. With those masculine clothes and the DA haircut, she'd probably resent any reference to her dubious femininity, so he might as well play along.

"Yes—*Ms.* Weldon. I write grant requests. I've come in response to an inquiry from a client. He's received information regarding some generous grants the foundation has recently made to certain institutions. In particular to several private mental hospitals engaged in research work, orphanages, and for studies on aging and its effects."

Anita Weldon's smile grew warmer than her mere professional one. "We're rather proud of the benefits that have come from our efforts in those areas. Which aspects are you specifically interested in?"

"I would like, if—if it is at all possible, to study the manner in which grant requests were written for the orphanages. My client is desirous of establishing a network of homes for runaway children who have, so to speak, orphaned themselves and have no desire to be reunited with their families." The Penetrator made a nervous, clutching gesture around the brim of his porkpie hat.

He hoped that it, along with his out-of-date charcoal suit, stiffly starched white shirt, polka-dot bow tie, and rimless, gold wire-temple glasses would complete the picture of a shy, somewhat esoteric academician who specialized in writing requests for foundation funds to further obscure social and cultural experiments. Anita Weldon's superior-seeming sniff of censure rewarded him with assurance of his success.

"We do not ordinarily make such information available, Mr. Miller. The needs, plans, and financial data of our clients is confidential." The Penetrator contrived to look dejected. "However—as I said, we are justifiably, I think, proud of our accomplishments in aiding such institutions. In light of that, I am sure I can assist you in the manner you wish with my superior's approval." She reached out a hand, slender fingers briefly touching Mark's arm. "Accompany me, if you please, we can find a less—public—place to go over the records you wish to see."

The Penetrator went with Anita Weldon and in fifteen minutes had made note of seven orphanages which had been the beneficiaries of Felder Foundation generosity. One in particular, in Salt Lake City, Utah, had been receiving grants on a regular basis over the past three years. He made note of all of them, their locations and nature of their facilities, thanked Ms. Weldon profusely, and departed.

\* \* \*

"What was it he wanted to know about?" a furious-faced David Felder demanded of Anita Weldon three hours later. She stood before Felder's desk, pale and visibly shaken.

"A-about the orphanages, Mr. Felder. This Miller person said he wrote grant requests and had a client who intended to open runaway shelters. I thought—in light of our work with the orphanages, we might look over whatever papers he sent in and maybe put this client to our own uses."

"Yes, yes. A good idea on the outside. I can see why you were so easily misled. What did this Miller look like?"

Anita gave Felder a description. When she finished, David Felder stabbed a button on his intercom. "Security? I want the tape from ten to eleven up here at once."

"Yes, sir. Will you need a videotape machine?"

"I have one of my own. Hurry it, will you?"

A technician arrived at the same time as the security guard bearing the tape record of persons entering and leaving One Felder Square during the hour from ten to eleven that morning. The young electronics tech put the cartridge into a Betamax set concealed by sliding panels in Felder's office. He turned on a recessed twenty-three-inch Curtis-Mathis color set and started the magnetic band rolling.

"There. Stop it on that man," Felder demanded some three minutes into the spool. "See? Do you all see him? I'll swear and be damned that this man is the Penetrator." He ordered the tape to roll again. When Mark departed, Felder stopped it again.

"Let me have the one from the foundation office as well," he instructed the guard. "While you're gone, I want to see this over again."

After a quick rewind, David Felder once more peered intently at the tall figure who walked into the lobby downstairs and disappeared into the elevator. "It is. It is him! I'm positive."

Ten minutes passed before the security man returned with another tape cartridge. He gave it to the technician, who inserted it in the Betamax. A moment of disorienting flashes and vague images came on first, then the hallway door opened and the same figure entered. Felder observed the entire visit with growing impatience, then thanked his employees and showed them out of his office.

"Send in Lake and Tilton," he curtly ordered his secretary.

"Yes, sir."

Lake and Tilton looked like a matched pair of linebackers for the Dallas Cowboys. Their brawn attracted attention, but also served to efficiently hide the bulge of shoulder holsters at each man's left armpit. They nodded at David Felder's greeting and took chairs.

"I want you to see this tape from security. Watch carefully the guy in the faggy-looking outfit. He isn't what he appears to be."

Without further comment, Felder turned on the videotape machine. After two run-throughs, he snapped off the TV set. "Well? What do you think?"

"He looks like that guy you sent out the special flier on, Mr. Felder," Patrick Lake responded.

Norman Tilton frowned a moment. "Yeah," he

reluctantly agreed. "He sure does resemble the Penetrator."

"It's him, damnit. Watch it again, then tell me if I'm not right. And he was here, right in this building this morning. Worse, he asked about a most sensitive subject. We can no longer tolerate such invasions. Once you're sure you can recognize him, I want you two to organize a search of the city for him. We have enough cops on the take to handle that during their regular patrol hours. Use some of them, along with our own men, to check all the hotels. When you locate where he's staying, put a stakeout there until he arrives."

"And when we find him?" Tilton inquired.

David Felder paused a moment, long, artistic fingers poised over his sensuous lips. "I think he should become the victim of another routine mugging. A fatal victim at that."

# 4

## AERIAL INCIDENT

When seen by day from the towering buildings
that surround them, the exquisite parks of New
York City—Pershing, the Sheep Meadow, in Central Park—seem like glowing green gems set in a
giant's concrete brooch.

At night they take on a sinister guise and with it
ominous names to fit their transformed reputa-
tions; Needle Park, Junkie Junction, Mugger
Gulch. Natives, and informed visitors, avoid the
immediate area of these threatening pieces of
real estate after dark. Unfortunately for Mark
Hardin, the most direct route from the restaurant,
where he had eaten dinner, back to his hotel took
him along one side of Central Park.

Long ago the city officials had given up trying to
maintain adequate lighting, so that the
Penetrator moved from pools of brightness into
stygian shadows. Three feet away, over the
curved spike-topped wall that separated the
park proper from the street, vandals had elimi-
nated every light globe and reduced the lush
vegetation to menacing mounds that suited well
the evil business done among them. Three figures,
only barely recognizable as human, detached

themselves from the undergrowth near a mid-block entranceway and stealthily rushed onto the sidewalk behind the Penetrator.

Mark Hardin sensed their presence instantly. He wondered at the accuracy of his intuition. Generally a person of his size was never selected by the cowardly scum who made their living by mugging citizens. Yet every instinct told Mark he was about to be mugged. Shoe leather whispered sibilantly on the pavement as the three young thugs closed in on him.

The Penetrator started to turn and immediately saw an Angelo youth and two blacks. One of the scumbags held a length of chain, studded with razor blades, while the other two had wicked-looking knives. The closest youth, mouth white froth-rimmed, spittle flying in his self-induced rage, yelled at him.

"Your wallet, motherfucker, let's have it now."

"Sure—sure. Take it easy with those knives, huh, fellas?" The Penetrator began to comply meekly enough by drawing a light tan leather wallet from his inside coat pocket.

This was going to be easy, Dino Rodriquez thought with relief. This turkey was going right along with them. Once he's dead, there'd be twice the smack that dude gave to line up the job. Cool, man. Nothin' to do then but stay spaced out for three days on that good stuff. Yeah—easy.

Dino Rodriquez failed to note one important item. His evaluation of the billfold contained one fatal error. It wasn't what it appeared to be. It was a Jackass Leather Company wallet holster for a High Standard .22 Magnum derringer.

The Penetrator's first bullet took Dino two inches below his woolly Afro and drove bone splinters ahead of its mushrooming shape deep into the young Puerto Rican's brain. The lights went out for Dino for the last time and he let the knife fall from suddenly numb fingers a second before his corpse hit the ground.

Even before Death reached out to claim Dino Rodriquez, the Penetrator's second shot sent a slug into Hector Gomez's open, screaming mouth. It burst through the back of that pink cavity and disconnected Hector's medulla oblongata from his spinal cord. Hector began to flop around on the sidewalk like a headless chicken.

Motivated by mindless terror, the third mugger, Gary Owens, attacked instead of running away. He shook his blond locks out of his face and leaped forward with his chain flail.

The Penetrator turned away from his assailant and bent low, body nearly parallel with the sidewalk, so that the razor-blade studded chain whooshed harmlessly past over his horizontal frame at the same moment he unleashed an *ushiro kekomi geri* rear thrust kick. The hard outer edge of his leather sole crashed into Gary's chest, snapped three ribs, and drove the air from the youthful criminal's lungs. Gasping, Gary staggered backward, bent forward at the waist. The Penetrator gave him no time to recover.

Mark stepped in on his opponent and drove his right knee upward at the same time he grasped Gary by the head and jerked the mugger down against his rising *hiza geri* knee kick.

A volcano of bright lights burst in Gary's head

and Mrs. Owens's little monster dropped out of the fight quicker than he had dropped out of school. His lips mashed and split when they came in contact with the concrete walk. The Penetrator looked quickly around, to discover the battle had ended.

In a car parked fifty yards down the street on the opposite side, Patrick Lake jolted out of his seat, one hand clawing at the butt of his Smith & Wesson Model 59.

"Christ," he cried to Norman Tilton. "That guy's a fuckin' avalanche."

Tilton had already cleared himself from behind the steering wheel and stood on the sidewalk. "It didn't go exactly like we planned it, I'll give you that."

"Let's blow the bastard up!" Lake yelled as he darted into the street, gun in hand, and ran toward the distant form of the Penetrator.

The Penetrator saw the blue black glow of Lake's Model 59 in the light of a distant streetlamp. Time for a new course of action, he decided. Mark dropped the empty .22 derringer into an outer coat pocket and drew his Star PD while Lake's first bullet zipped past his head and smashed itself against the wall of Central Park. The Star barked fiercely and spat a 185-grain, .45-caliber Federal Jacketed Hollow Point at the charging man, now only ten feet away.

Mark's slug took Lake in the left side of his groin. He grunted in pain and fell to the macadam street surface. *Damn,* the Penetrator thought, this new PD had a tendency to group low and right. In his haste he had forgotten to compensate for it. Then he dived for the gutter when Norman Tilton entered the fight.

Three fast shots, spaced so closely together that they sounded nearly like one, chipped concrete from the curb near the Penetrator's shoulder. Then the wounded man got back in the battle.

Two sharp reports came from the 9mm pistol in Patrick Lake's hand. A shard of lead and small chunks of blacktop made tiny cuts on the Penetrator's face. Mark cooly returned fire with far greater accuracy than his would-be killer.

A big .45 round entered Patrick Lake's left eyeball, exploded out the side of his head, and brought with it a gout of brain matter, blood, and bone fragments. Lake flopped onto his back and violently kicked out his remaining sparks of life.

Right then Norman Tilton decided he would rather be a live loser than the dead follower of suicidal orders.

The Penetrator heard a car door slam while he still searched for his second assailant. The engine of the Buick Skylark roared to life and Norman Tilton left a blue haze of rubber smoke behind when he raced away from the curb and disappeared down the street. To Mark's right, he saw movement.

Gary Owens had regained consciousness and crawled feebly away to the sanctuary of darkness inside the park. He saw the Penetrator looking at him, a big, ugly automatic pistol in one hand, and he made a weak gesture of surrender.

"Hey, man. Peace, huh? I—I figure I'm lucky to get out of this with a few broke ribs and a squashed face. Look—I—uh, wanna get my shit together. Maybe take a job, huh? There has to be a better way to make a living than this."

"You've got it right for once. What set you on me?"

Gary Owens looked into the street, at the corpse of Patrick Lake. There was no reason for keeping quiet. "That one. He hired us to hit you. Was gonna pay us in high-grade heroin. Said we could turn it on the streets for heavy bread or stay high for a week. Funny, but it don't even sound like a good idea now." Sirens wailed in the distance, coming at them from three directions. Owens glanced about nervously and started to crawl again.

"That's right, keep going that way, asshole. I'm going the other. Maybe neither one of us will get caught," the Penetrator growled. The street punks, the muggers, saw themselves as tough, the meanest machines around. This one had just found out he didn't know what mean was. It might do the kid some good, Mark thought, if he kept up the badass pose until the injured youth fled into the park. He went to Lake's body and searched the dead man.

In a wallet, Mark found an ID card that gave Lake's name and indicated that he worked as a security guard for Grace Bank.

From his room the Penetrator called Dan Griggs. He briefed the Justice Department man on the shooting incident and then filled him in on his day's activities. He concluded with his plans for the next morning.

"I'm going to Salt Lake City. I'll fly out tomorrow."

"Why there?"

"I'm a little curious about why the Felder Foundation is endowing orphanages. Remember, Cottler tried to say something about orphanages on that tape."

"You going hot?"

"Sure. I'll use those dandy credentials you fixed up for me to ship my goodies in my luggage."

"Sounds like you expect trouble."

"I always do, Dan, I always do."

At eleven the next morning, Mark boarded a TWA direct flight from La Guardia to Salt Lake City. Nestled in his left armpit was the flat bulk of his plastic $CO_2$-powered dart gun, Ava. Lacking any bulk of metal, the deadly little weapon could pass through all security screens. Mark found his seat and strapped in.

During the usual preliminaries about oxygen masks and escape hatches, the Penetrator studied his fellow passengers. Three of them, in different parts of the aircraft, appeared unusually ill at ease. They seemed to fidget and cast nervous glances at the cabin attendants. If it didn't sound unduly melodramatic, the Penetrator thought, he'd be willing to swear the three persons knew each other and that they were up to something.

A few minutes after takeoff, when the Fasten Seat Belts sign went off, one of the dark-skinned, Latin-looking men rose and walked into the first-class compartment. He stopped one of the stewardesses and spoked earnestly to her, though his words could not be heard over the jet roar, and then grasped her firmly around one upper arm. He turned the uniformed, trim-waisted young woman and urged her forward, toward the door to the flight deck. The other two, an olive-skinned young woman and another Latino man, got from their seats and stood in the aisle. The girl took the intercom mike in one hand while she and her partner produced handguns.

"All right, ever'body," she announced in heavily accented Engligh. "Sit back and enjoy your flight. We are going to Havana. *¡Viva Fidel! ¡Viva Cuba!*'

Childish voices, high and piping, sounded with gleeful exuberance on the sprawling playground to one side and across the back of the Carstairs Foundling Home in Salt Lake City, Utah. A volleyball, like a small white moon, floated over a net and the two teams of girls yelled shrilly, caught up in the excitement of the game. Half a dozen boys took turns knocking fly balls to a foreshortened outfield and another cluster of youngsters gathered around a wide circle, faces serious in contemplation of a tense marble contest. The boys faces wore looks of pained irritation over the ease with which a black-haired, impish-featured little girl was beating them. One child, though, did not share the mid-morning recess activities.

Dennis Roberts stood before the desk of the home's director. Arnold Meeks, his bald pate shiny with perspiration, glowered at the errant boy. "This isn't the first time you have failed to attend class, Dennis. I must warn you, punishment comes swift and sure around here. Dr. DiFalco tells me you didn't go to his social studies class this morning. Do you have even the most simpleminded reason why?"

"I—I don't like it," Dennis offered in weak defense.

"We all do things we don't like, boy," the director fired back. He studied the short, sturdy lad standing in front of him.

Dennis had a dusting of freckles over his short nose and high, rosy cheeks, and his longish blond hair partly covered his ears. His dark brown eyes glowed with intelligence and an understanding usually found only in adults. Meeks recalled that the boy had a sweet, engaging smile, but he could at times, as he did now, put on the somber face of a cardinal. He had been a problem, in one way or another, since he'd first come to the institution. Director Meeks shook his head sadly and pursed his thick lips.

"Dennis, Dennis. You don't seem to appreciate all that we are trying to do for you here at the Carstairs Home."

"Exactly what *is it* that you're trying to do for me?" Dennis asked with the cool incisiveness of a much older person.

"Don't be impudent, young man!" Meeks snapped. "All right, since you see fit to flaunt the rules, you shall be restricted from all playground activities for a week, confined to your room during recess periods for the same time, and no television privilege tonight. Now go and think to yourself about becoming a more cooperative citizen."

Head down, mouth set in an obstinate line, Dennis scuffed the toes of his shoes while he walked along the hallway and up the stairs to the dormitory wing. Oh how he wished he could run around with his shoes off. His shirt, too. Dennis remembered back two years to before his folks had died and he'd become an orphan. He used to spend every summer barefoot and shirtless, in cut-offs and swim trunks until he grew so brownly tanned that when he examined the unexposed skin of his rear end it seemed to glow in the mirror with an unnatural whiteness. Now he only got to go barefoot in the room he shared with Wes and Devon and in the shower, and the little tan he had gotten during the few hours each day the home allowed the boys to go without shirts over the past summer had already faded to an unhealthy, doughy color. Dennis threw open the door to his empty room and entered.

He flung himself on his bed and for a minute thought about crying. But, hell, a guy didn't do those sorts of things when he was eleven years old. He felt mad. Damn good and mad at that old fatso Meeks, and at Dr. DiFalco. God, how he hated those silly classes. They didn't teach anything. At least nothing *he* wanted to learn. Social studies? Who cared about the cultural struggle in Angola or how a people's court worked in Russia? Maybe—maybe he'd run away. Could he get away with it? There'd been that thing on TV about kids young as nine and ten running away from home and disappearing forever. And they came from familes that loved and cared about them. Could be he could do it—if he ever got the chance. A single large tear escaped from each of Dennis's tightly squinted eyelids.

* * *

"Hijacked! HIJACKED!" a fat woman sitting across the aisle from the Penetrator shrieked. "Somebody do something."

"Shut up, *señora,* or I'll tap you on the head with this pistol, no?" the grinning Latino bent low to tell her.

The woman's face went pale and her eyelids fluttered. She screwed up her pouting mouth into a rubbery circle and emitted a fluttery moan. Then she went slack and managed an old-fashioned faint.

"Now see here," a man cried indignantly. "What the hell do you people think you're doing? I have an important appointment in Salt Lake. I must be there by this afternoon."

"You are going to be a little late, *gringo.* Now sit back down and shut up."

"Who are you people? Why are you doing this to us?"

The young Cuban answered the panicky woman's inquiry. "I am Maria Sandoval and this is Juan Pedro Ortiz. Our comrade who has gone forward to take command of the flight deck is Manuel Escobar. We came to this country with the so-called refugees because we wanted to see what *los Estados Unidos del Norte* were like. We do not like it and we wanted to go to our homeland. But—no money. So we take this airplane and return to our beloved Cuba and our benefactor, Fidel."

"Shit!" a man three rows back of Mark exploded. "Shit, shit, shit.

For twenty minutes the Boeing 727 sped through the skies, headed due south, with the deep green fields and rolling hills of Virginia below. The passengers, depending on their nature, reacted in differing ways, from grumbling anger to near hysteria. The two armed Cubans wached them carefully. At one point, the girl, Maria Sandoval, instructed the cabin attendants to pass out coffee and soft drinks—no liquor. When the diverted flight had been on course to Miami for a refueling stop for half an hour, the Penetrator undid his seat belt and rose, bent slightly to avoid the overhead luggage compartment, and started across the other two seats to the aisle.

"You there," Juan Ortiz demanded peremptorily. "Where do you think you're going, *gringo?*"

"I—ah—have to go to the . . ." Mark Hardin gestured toward the aft portion of the airliner, were the rest rooms were located.

"That can wait."

"No—no it can't. I would make a terrible mess. It's the . . ." the Penetrator whispered the word, *"touristas."*

"Ahaha! I understand now. You can eat their food in New York, but don't drink the *gringos'* water, heh? All right. You can go. I will accompany you to see there is no, how you say, funny business."

"You mean—inside there?"

"*¿Ciertamente no!* I will wait outside."

The Penetrator made his way down the aisle with the gun-toting Cuban behind him. He entered the small cubical and latched the door. He rattled the toilet seat and made noises appropriate to his professed purpose. The he drew Ava from his left armpit and checked the load. He stripped the first round, a sleeper dart loaded with a powerful tranquilizer in a suspension of

DMSO. The red-tipped missile below it was armed with curarine and would bring nearly instant death. He didn't want one of the hijackers coming around while he had two others to face.

Outside the small compartment, Juan Ortiz braced himself against the bulkhead. The 727 had encountered an area of light turbulence which made standing unassisted difficult. His thoughts sped from his present situation to his beloved homeland, Cuba.

What a beautiful island. One well worth the blood of a patriot—or his martyred death. His father, a *campesiño* who had fled the drudgery of the cane fields to join Fidel in the Sierra Maestra the same year little Juan turned twelve, had fought bravely for the revolution and had died horribly at the hands of Batista's brutal batallions two short months before Dr. Castro had victoriously led his ragged army into Havana. Juan had grown up in the shadow of his father's martyrdom. When he reached the age for the university, something guaranteed him by his high intelligence and his father's sacrifice for Fidel's cause, he went, instead, to special schooling. He emerged a member of the National Security Bureau, Cuban Intelligence. When the decision had been made to shovel out the unwanted; the aged, ill, homosexuals, petty thieves, and political dissidents from the prisons, along with a large enough quantity of healthy, useful citizens to give protective coloration, over fifty BNS agents were chosen to go along. A garbage run, Juan's superior officer had called it. Multiple benefits were expected to derive from the intelligence personnel included.

First, they were to foment unrest among the refugees in the relocation camps during the processing phase. Second, they were to observe life in the hated United States and make full reports on all they encountered. Thirdly, when their information gathering had been completed, they were to make their way back home in some showy manner, denouncing the Americans and thus causing them embarrassment. The most spectacular way, of course, would be airplane hijackings. Juan had been surprised to discover that Maria Sandoval, a girl with whom he had grown up, was also an agent. But then, they had been "sleepers" even at home among their fellow Cubans. Each of them knew the code names and locations of five other operatives. Juan had thought it ironic that two of those he shared in common with Maria's list had been living in Salt Lake City, the destination of this aircraft prior to their taking it over. He wondered when those two would make their break for home and how. Ah, to serve your country and do it well.

It would mean promotion for him, of course. And—he might find time to get closer to Maria. She'd been a pretty little thing when they'd been in school together. The door to the rest room suddenly opened, interrupting Juan's thoughts. The *gringo* stood there, a frightened look on his face.

"There's—there's something wrong in here." I think it might be dangerous to the airplane," the *gringo* told Juan.

"Let me see." Juan stepped through the opening without thinking.

The Penetrator shot Juan Ortiz with the deadly poison dart in Ava. The Cuban BNS agent went into convulsions and Mark grabbed him, easing the dying man onto the toilet seat. He took the pistol from Juan's hand, braced himself, and stepped out into the aisle.

Maria Sandoval had seen Juan enter the rest room compartment, and now, when the *gringo* came out alone, she knew something had gone terribly wrong. Then she caught sight of the pistol in the tall, dark-complected man's hand and she brought up her own weapon.

She fired at the Penetrator from point-blank range.

# 5
# PRYING EYES

The Penetrator dropped like a sack of stones.

Maria's bullet smashed into the unused liquor service cart, shattered glass and mingled Chivas Regal with Beefeaters' gin, Smirnoff vodka, and fragmented bottles of Jack Daniels black. Feeling momentarily helpless and exposed, Mark realized that the distance was too great down the aisle of the 727 for him to use Ava. Passengers, both men and women, screamed in fear. The Penetrator took aim with the 9mm Radom pistol he had taken from Juan Ortiz.

He had to make his bullet placement the best ever. He sighted carefully, despite his feeling of zero lag time. The Radom boomed loudly that close to the floor and Maria spun away from where she stood to crash into the dividing partition between the main cabin and the first-class section. The slug smashed out through Maria's shoulder blade and drove through the divider. It made a loud crack when it hit the high-impact plastic of the overhead luggage compartment and ended its deadly path embedded in a thick, leather-bound book on corporate law that rested

47

in an old-fashioned satchel-top briefcase of a first-class passenger. Maria slumped down into a sitting position.

A large red stain spread wetly from her right shoulder. She emitted a small squeal of pain through tightly clenched teeth and toppled over to curl into a fetal ball, then she slowly rocked to the rhythmic waves of her pain. The sound of the shots pierced the constant background noise and alerted Manuel Escobar on the flight deck.

Escobar threw open the door that separated the cockpit from the rest of the airplane. Immediately he spotted Mark lying in the aisle. He threw a hasty shot that ricocheted off a seat arm and punched a small hole in the skin of the aircraft. A whistling shriek warned the Penetrator of rapid, if not fatally explosive, decompression due to the altitude. He had to finish this and quickly.

Mark took careful aim and shot Escobar in the chest. Mark's bullet went in at a low angle, ripped upward and shredded Escobar's right lung, snapped his clavicle, and turned ninety degrees. When the slug exited Escobar's body, it struck the thick door of a microwave oven in the stewardess forward station and expended the last of its energy. It fell soundlessly onto the aisle carpet. The big man staggered backward and tried to bring his own handgun to bear.

The Penetrator fired again.

A copper-jacketed, round-nose 9mm slug hit Escobar half an inch above his navel. It sliced through intestines, pulped his left kidney, changed direction, and shattered a vertebra before lodging in the honeycomb structure of the bulkhead behind him. Escobar doubled over, quite dead, to the floor. Two women passengers shrieked like a chorus of police sirens. The Penetrator came to his feet and rushed forward to the flight deck. All the while, his mind worked on how he could extricate himself from this situation.

"I'm a federal officer," Mark explained, showing the crew his fake ID. "Contact the ATC who's handling you and tell him the hijack is over. We will continue on to Salt Lake City. Don't let anyone divert you elsewhere. Tell them I'm aboard and in charge. Then get on your company frequency and inform your people of what has happened." Mark paused and smiled at the pilot. "The airplane's yours again, captain."

"Uh—well, ah, thanks, buddy."

"I want to question the survivor and you'd better take us down below ten thousand. There's a hole in the skin and we're leaking pressure." Screams from the passenger compartment added veracity to Mark's words. He turned to see the familiar yellow-foam-rubber face cones of the oxygen system dangling from their containers at the ends of clear plastic hose. A minor difficulty, the Penetrator thought. He had a much bigger one, despite his ploy with the crew. How could he avoid the prying eyes and pointed questions of officialdom and the press once they got down?

"I won't do it! You can't make me," Dennis Roberts shouted in defiance of Arnold Meeks's ultimatum. "Who wants to study the 'History of the People's World Struggle toward Socialism'? Why can't we learn American history like in a real school?"

Arnold Meeks's hand flashed out and he

slapped Dennis solidly on one cheek. The blow rocked the small boy backward, and he was saved from falling only by the hard-handed grasp of Dr. Treavor DiFalco. DiFalco's fingers bit painfully into the flesh of Dennis's upper arm and he shook the youngster with controlled force.

Director Meeks's voice seemed to thunder in Dennis's ears. "This is the second time today that you've skipped a class. You've spoken rudely and made an obscene gesture to Dr. DiFalco. Why are you so intractable, boy?"

"You've got to understand, Dennis, that we know what's best for you," Dr. DiFalco injected in a reasoning tone. "You are a part of the proletarian struggle for world liberation and, as such, you must accept your place in life."

"Yes, Dennis," Meeks interjected, somewhat calmed. "Dr. DiFalco is right. You are being prepared for a part in a mighty effort that will free from oppression millions of little boys and girls like yourself all over the world."

"I don't want to go all over the world. I want to live here. I am an American."

"You are an ungrateful, reactionary little beast is what you are," Meeks snapped, his control gone again. "Very well. If you persist in your counterrevolutionary attitudes, you must take the punishment. Except for classes and meals, you are restricted to your room for a month. No television privileges for two weeks. If you miss a single study session, class meeting, or drill period, you shall be whipped." A light glowed behind Arnold Meeks's eyes. "Speaking of whippings, you have one coming now."

Dennis's eyes grew wide and he struggled to break free of DiFalco's grip. "No," he pleaded. "Please, noooo."

"Drop your trousers, boy," the director of the Carstairs Foundling Home commanded while he took a wide leather strap down from the wall behind his desk.

Dennis blushed a light pink. "N-not in front of you two."

"Down with them or we'll have 'em off you before you know what happened."

Treavor DiFalco's large, hard right hand swung downward and he tugged at the snap-fastener of Dennis's thin, corduroy shorts. The catch parted and the zipper spread open. He drew down the boy's trousers, exposing his bare buttocks. Arnold Meeks came from behind his desk, a look of sensual anticipation on his face. In one fist he flicked the flexible paddle. He raised it on high and brought it down smartly on Dennis's naked flesh.

Dennis bit the inside of his lower lip until it bled in order to keep from crying out or letting tears flow in front of his tormentors. The youngster had a streak of stubborness that matched his high intelligence and he succeeded in not losing control during the whipping.

Afterward, while he limped toward his room, twin salty streams ran wetly down his cheeks. Gasping back his sobs, he swallowed his humiliation until he threw himself on his bed and let it all escape in inconsolable anguish. When his misery subsided, Dennis coldly and calmly began to plan his escape.

* * *

A stewardess opened the forward loading door of the 727 and three FBI men, guns in hand, rushed into the airplane.

"Where are the hijackers?" the man in the lead demanded.

"The two dead ones are back in the rest room," the Penetrator informed the agents. "You'll need an ambulance for the girl there." Mark pointed to Maria Sandoval, who huddled in a first-class seat.

"Two dead?" the FBI man asked wonderingly. "How did that happen?"

"I'm Greg Miller with Dan Griggs' section. We've been on this from the start." He drew the agent in charge, who introduced himself as Paul Brown, off to one side and began the elaborate explanation he had schemed up during the remainder of the flight to hopefully escape too close a look by the Feds.

"Look, Paul, I've interrogated the woman, Maria Sandoval. These three were part of a Cuban intelligence operation. She gave me the names of five others, two here in Salt Lake. That's why I ordered the plane to come here. These BNS operatives were planted by Castro to create similar incidents to this hijacking. We've been on this from the start, like I told you, because the plan involves some prominent crime figures. But—I'm out here alone. I'd appreciate it if you got the Sandoval woman off to the hospital, under guard naturally, and came along with me on the raid to scoop up this pair in Salt Lake City. We'll have to move fast because the press will be onto the hijacking and the suspects might try to make a break. Are you game?"

Thoughts of promotion, or at least honorable

mention in his personnel jacket, formed behind Paul Brown's smooth, tanned forehead, and his pale blue eyes glowed with excitement.

"You bet I am. How soon can we leave?"

"Soon as you have everything ready. I'm going to pick up my luggage, and a car that's supposed to be waiting for me and we can go in two vehicles."

"You're on," Brown enthused.

Fifteen minutes later, the Penetrator led the two-car cavalcade out the sweeping entrance-way to the Salt Lake City airport. In the back seat rested his luggage. He headed south to I-10, then into the heart of town, where, at an interchange he swung to the southeast. Five minutes after that he took an off-ramp that gave access to a short, two-block commercial district and then to quiet residential streets. Mark blocked the driveway of 3275 Holcomb Street with his rental car and the FBI unit stopped half a block down. Mark extracted his Star PD from his suitcase and noticed a flicker of motion behind the thick drapes drawn across a large picture window. Paul Brown and another FBI man joined him at the car.

"Well, let's take 'em," Brown announced eagerly.

"Did you send a man around back?"

Brown looked at the Penetrator with chagrin. "Oh, shit, I never thought of it. Looks like you're it, Jonesey," he told the other agent.

"Give him two minutes to get in place and we'll make our move," the Penetrator instructed.

A minute crept past. Again the Penetrator noticed furtive motion at the center split of the drapes, and from the attached garage came the sound of what could have been a trunk lid being slammed. The second hand continued to stutter forward on Mark's Omega pilot's chronograph. A heavy sigh from Paul Brown broke the silence.

"That's it. Let's go," the Penetrator commanded. He stepped from the car and started up the walkway beside the FBI man.

Paul Brown rang the doorbell twice, paused, then pounded solidly on the heavey wooden panel. "Mr. Garcia? Mrs. Garcia? Are you there?" Silence greeted his call.

"Let me try. ¿Señor, Señora Garcia? ¡Abierta la puerta, por favor!'

"We're federal officers, Mr. Garcia. Open the door!"

A burst of automatic-weapon fire answered Paul Brown's demand.

The stream of slugs crashed through the corner of the picture window and broke into shards an undecorated, red-brown clay pot that held a cactus garden. The fragment flew close past Agent Brown's shoulder. He rapidly ducked, his face pale and looking a little sheepish. The Penetrator pressed the attack.

Mark put two .45 slugs into the door beside the lock case and gave the panel a solid kick. It flew open and Brown dived in, did a roll, and came up with his revolver pointed into the living room. Another blast from the chattergun turned painted drywall into a cloud of gray-white dust an inch above Brown's head. He flattened out and returned fire.

The Penetrator swung his Star to the right and put five fast .45 slugs through the thin, uninsulated inside wall at a point where he judged the machine gunner to be standing. A man's voice cried out, a woman screamed, and the sound of a body striking furniture, then the carpeted floor, came to Mark's ears. He stepped closer to the entranceway to the living room.

"¡Por amor de Dios, no más!" Mrs. Garcia cried, then repeated in English. "For the love of God, no more."

Agent Brown came to his feet as the woman staggered into the hallway. He kept his .357 Magnum trained on her while the Penetrator removed a .380 Beretta from the limp clasp of her left hand.

"Mrs. Garcia, you are under arrest for espionage against the United States."

"No. No. Not me. I-I had nothing to do with it. It was him. *Yo no soy una come cuenta.*" Her earnest protest of innocence lapsed into Spanish, without becoming the least bit more believable.

"I know you don't want to be the fall guy," the Penetrator responded in the same language. "Tell us all about it and no harm will come to you."

Slowly, she began to respond in broken English and Spanish. Mark walked on past her into the living room. He bent to examine Raul Garcia.

Blood flowed from two wounds, one in Garcia's left upper arm and the other in his lower abdomen, near the left hip. Good shooting, the Penetrator congratulated himself, particularly in the blind.

"This one's still alive," he called to Brown. "I'll call for an ambulance. The Penetrator went to the telephone and dialed the number the FBI man gave him from the hallway. While Mark passed instructions to the ambulance service, Raul Garcia regained consciousness. He reached slowly and cautiously to the waistband of his trousers and pulled out a Smith & Wesson Model 59.

"Now you die, *gringo cabrón!*" he yelled at Mark.

Unaware that her husband had drawn his hideout gun, Luisa Garcia shouted from out in the hall. "*¡No le creas lo que dice, él es un buche y pluma!*"

The Penetrator's .45 slug hit Garcia in his right shoulder. The heavy bullet smashed him backward, jerked the pistol from his hand the pain of the new wound drove Garcia back into unconsciousness.

"I pay attention to anyone who threatens to kill me," the Penetrator replied with dry, gallows humor. "And he got another bullet for his efforts, bluff or not." Mark stepped out of the room to be with Brown and the Garcia woman. Agent Jones joined them from the back of the house.

"Nobody out that way. I heard a lot of shooting."

"Yeah, Jonesey. Garcia had a submachine gun. He threw a couple of bursts at us," Brown explained.

Jones looked at his superior's condition, jacket ripped slightly at one shoulder seam, scrape marks on both knees, and a large wet stain at his crotch. "You spill a glass of water or somethin', Brown?"

"Go screw yourself, Jonesey. Gettin' shot at with chatter gun is scary."

"I'll second that," the Penetrator added tactfully. "Why don't you have Jonesey here take Mrs. Garcia down to the office in your car? You can wait with Garcia for the ambulance and I'll follow Jones in. You guys can do the report."

"And get the credit?"

"Why not, Brown? I'm hot on the rest of these scumbags."

"Okay. I'll see you at the office after I get Garcia booked into the prison ward at the hospital."

"Fine. Shall we go, Jones?"

"Yes, sir."

Agent Jones, with his prisoner firmly handcuffed in the back seat of the FBI sedan, pulled from the curb and headed toward downtown Salt Lake City. The Penetrator eased out into traffic and followed him for six blocks, then turned off and drove away.

His finesse had worked and he had avoided all the prying eyes.

# 6

## SAFETY FIRSTS

"Here you are, Mr. Miller, Room 216. That's the building immediately behind the office, ground floor on the pool side." The young motel clerk handed the Penetrator a key and flashed a professional smile. Then he produced a large manila envelope. "There is a package for you too, sir."

"Thank you." Mark noticed the handwritten address and canceled postage stamps. At least Dan Griggs had not used a penalty envelope. The superscription, "Postage Paid by the United States Government" and printed DOJ return would not have done his new cover ID a bit of good. He took the package with him to his rental Aspen and drove to the slot in front of 216. He carried in his luggage, secured the door, and adjusted the temperature control; motel maids always left them too hot or too cold. Then he opened the package.

Dan had come through. He was now Greg Miller, an employee of the state of Utah. A safety inspector for the Department of Education. With the ID card came a letter of authorization to inspect certain private orphan facilities, including the Carstairs Foundling Home. Little of the afternoon remained after his day with the hijackers and Cuban agents. He called the Carstairs director and set an appointment for the next morning. Then the Penetrator spent the rest of the sunlight hours at the pool, swimming brisk laps and soaking up sun.

"*How do you do,* Mr. Miller," Arnold Meeks enthused while he wrung the Penetrator's hand early the next morning on the front steps of the Carstairs Foundling Home. A big, barnlike structure, done in a depressing shade of buff with black trim and iron grillwork bars on the windows, the "U" shaped building had an imposing, almost intimidating, presence.

"We're always happy to cooperate with you state people. Always. Will you come into my office or would you like to start your inspection?"

"Let's take a turn around the outside of the building first. I'd like to get a look at the hydrant fittings."

"The fire department did that last week, Mr. Miller."

"*They* represent the city, Mr. Meeks," the Penetrator responded somewhat snippily.

"Very well." Meeks led the way, chattering volubly about how it was his insistence that institution maintained the absolute highest standards. A group of junior-high-aged children, boys and girls, jogged past in formation, counting cadence like a platoon of basic trainees.

"Good for their lungs and circulation," Meeks added to his string of superlatives by way of explanation. The Penetrator pretended to make careful notes regarding the location and condition of hydrants that protruded from the tan-colored walls.

"Are these outlets on the same water line with the sprinkler system?"

"No. Separate, of course."

"Excellent." Mark studied the long, three-story sideface of the building. "I see there are no bars on these windows."

"Certainly not. Fire regulations, you know."

They returned to the front of the orphanage and entered. Down a long, dimly lighted corridor, Meeks ushered the Penetrator into his office. He arranged a chair near his desk, ordered coffee over the intercom, and placed his rotund bulk in a large, leather swivel chair behind a bare width of richly glowing mahogany.

"Are the health certificates of your kitchen workers up to date? And are they trained in how to handle grease fires?"

"Naturally."

"How often do you hold fire drills?"

"Every two weeks—on different days each time."

"Your teaching staff consists of certified people?"

"Yes, yes, of course they are."

"Are they trained in CPR?"

"Yes."

"You have a full-time duty nurse?"

"And a doctor who visits twice a week and is on call twenty-four hours a day for emergencies."

"Good. I see." The Penetrator was winging it and he knew it. He had no idea what a real state safety inspector would ask, so he tried to fake it with as broad a spectrum of questions as he could devise.

"When was your last termite inspection?"

"Last spring." Meeks sought to speed up the unwanted inspection. "Will you want to see the classrooms?"

"Yes, of course."

"We can go now then."

In the first classroom, the sullen, suspicious eyes of fourteen youngsters turned on the visitors when they entered. It was a study period and the Penetrator could gain no idea of subject matter from the open books and spiral note pads that lay on each child's desk. At the suggestion of Director Meeks, they moved on to another room, where a math class was in progress. The Penetrator hesitated here long enough to give the impression that he wanted to make sure the exit light worked and the fire extinguisher was in the proper place. He checked the aisle width with a metal tape, then signaled that they could leave.

"Do you have a chemistry lab?"

"Yes. In a separate, concrete-block building."

Further along the hall a large map of the island of Cuba had been pulled down over the blackboard. Eleven children gazed listlessly at the tip of a pointer that the teacher held on the Sierra Maestras. One boy, about eleven or twelve Mark guessed, seemed totally uninterested in the subject. He ran nervous, nail-bitten fingers through his longish blond hair and doodled on his notebook, drawing pictures of dragons and space ships and small American flags. The lecture proceeded without interruption by the observers' entrance.

"During the Batista regime, the social order of Cuba was sharply divided into two classes. The few, rich and powerful, controlled everything while the struggling masses, the *campesiños* as they were called, existed in a near serfdom hardly better than the Middle Ages. When the liberation came," the pointer moved down out of the mountains, toward Havana.

"Dr. Castro and his heroic freedom fighters marched into Havana to a tumultuous welcome by the oppressed *campeseños*. Since that time, Cuba has known a stability and prosperity unequaled anywhere in the Western Hemisphere. The people are happy and content and sincerely work toward spreading the benefits of their Marxist Socialist system to their brothers in Latin America."

The Penetrator shot a startled, disbelieving glance at Arnold Meeks. What sort of bullshit was this? The Cuban economy was a shambles. Shortages abounded and the sugar refineries were breaking down for lack of technicians. The support of Castro's puppet government daily became a greater burden on his master, the Soviet Union. The refugee-release program had provided a temporary lessening of strain, but since then matters only grew worse. Lately the Penetrator had been intercepting broadcasts from a station calling itself Radio Free Cuba. The content of those programs, highly critical of the Castro regime, had to be having an effect on internal order. He turned to Meeks, spoke in a whisper.

"Is that guy for real?"

"Oh, granted, that isn't exactly the way the state

curriculum for history goes, but the man's an absolute genius. Dr. Treavor DiFalco. He came highly recommended. He formerly ran a think tank for the *Société Internationale d'Élite*. Most prestigious, as I'm sure you know. After all, in a world like we live in, all things are relative, aren't they? He may sound a bit biased, but he manages to make the issues clear before the end of the course."

"Perhaps it's personal, an overreaction, but I had the feeling he was doing an excessive job of singing the praises of Castro and his fellow Communists."

"My, we are a conservative state here in Utah, aren't we? Shall we go?"

Their whispered conversation had not been quiet enough to be missed by Dennis Roberts. The Penetrator saw the blond-headed boy direct a beaming, almost affectionate smile toward him as they left the room.

After a quick review of two more classrooms, Arnold Meeks led his visitor to the gymnasium. He waved an expansive arm at the highly polished wooden floor of the basketball court and at one end of the building a set of weight machines. His voice vibrated with pride.

"We place a great deal of importance on physical conditioning. After all, these children have suffered considerable trauma. The shocks of life are quite harsh for orphans. Physical strength builds self-confidence, which should aid them well when they leave the institution."

"Most commendable," the Penetrator replied.

"We have installed nonskid strips in the shower rooms and the locker rooms. The benches and wall lockers are bolted down to prevent accients. That's about all, unless you want to inspect the kitchen and the dormitory wings."

"I don't think that will be necessary, Mr. Meeks. Those things are more the province of the child-welfare people."

"Fine, then, fine. Shall we return to my office?"

A click of high heels interrupted any answer from Mark Hardin. He and Meeks turned to see the silhouetted form of a trim, well-proportioned young woman approaching, a slim-line attaché case in her left hand.

"Mr. Meeks?" a melodious voice spoke in inquiry. The Penetrator's face tightened under a sudden flash of tension and surprise. He knew that voice. "Your secretary said I might find you here." The speaker closed the distance and gave both men a friendly smile.

"I'm Mrs. Dillon, Angie Dillon."

"How do you do, Mrs. Dillon?" Meeks greeted. "What's the nature of your visit?"

"I'm an attendance supervisor with the state Department of Education."

"We seem to be overrun with inspectors this morning. Are you acquainted with Mr. Miller here?"

A slight shadow of puzzled frown rippled across Angie's brow. "No, I don't believe so."

"Different offices, I'm afraid," the Penetrator explained in a casual, offhand manner. "I'd certainly not forget Mrs. Dillon, *had I met her before.*" Mark noted with relief that Angie had picked up on the import behind his heavy emphasis on the final words. She even managed to produce a mild blush.

"That's very kind of you, Mr. Miller. You're in? . . ."

"Safety."

"That's right. I see. Well, ah, perhaps I should come back later?"

"No, not at all. We were finished with my inspection. Go ahead and conclude your business with Mr. Meeks and perhaps we can have lunch together and talk shop?"

"I'd like that. All right. We'll do it."


"What in the name of heaven are you doing here, Mark?" Angie asked the Penetrator an hour later. They had located themselves in an isolated booth at a Sambo's Restaurant not far from the Carstairs Foundling Home. Mild irritation, along with curiosity and deep, abiding love, shared Angie's expression.

"The same thing I'm always doing. Tell me about you working for the state."

"It's for real, Mark. I—it all happened suddenly. I had this opportunity, more pay, better position, so I quit teaching in Coalville and moved here. The kids weren't too happy about it at first, and I don't particularly like the big city way of life, but career advancement is important. Now, give, what are you doing here?"

"It's all—up in the breeze. All ravelings and nothing to tie the strings together. Fill me in on what the state truant officer has to do with that Carstairs place and then I might have something that makes sense."

They paused while the waitress came and took their order, then Angie explained. "A lot I got from

...r my efforts. That man is slipperier than ...garten paste. What I came out on, the state ha... an overflow of youngsters in its institutions. Some of them are farmed out to private orphanages. Carstairs has—or had—some ten of them. Three of those seem to have totally disappeared over the last summer; Loren Chase, Robbie Fenton, and Petey Vail. The record checks are only now catching up to that fact."

"How do you mean? Runaways?"

"Simply that they're gone. No class-progress reports—that's a fancy, administrative euphemism for report cards—no health certificates. They've not been reported as run away from the home. In fact, Arnold Meeks claims they had never been there, although he signed vouchers for their state support money. It's—like they no longer exist. Not physically present, not in the hospital, no bodies at the morgue, no clue. And that's not the only such place we've been checking into."

"Oh? Go on. Who are the others?"

"Is this what you're working on, Mark?"

"You tell me first, then I'll tell you."

Angie crinkled her brow, forming a deep line between her russet eyebrows. "Oh, damn. All right. There's the Baylor Boy's Ranch outside Provo, the Queen of Angels Missionary School near Moab, and Carter's Youth Hostel just north of here in Bountiful. There are a couple more that are close to coming under investigation."

"I will be damned. You have kids disappearing from institutions that get a lot of their funding from the Felder Foundation and I have a man whose dying words indicated some connection between orphanages and the SIE."

"What are you talking about?"

"You know about Walter Cottler being murdered?" Angie nodded and the Penetrator went on. "What didn't get released to the press was that Cottler was working on a seven-part special report on the *Société Internationale d'Élite,* and while his killers were still in his office he managed to turn on hidden tape recorder. His last words were about orphanages."

Angie pursed her lips and worry creased her brow. A long silence held until after the waitress brought their sandwiches and iced tea. "What has the SIE to do with it? Isn't it some sort of government advisory council?"

"The SIE is no part of the government, at least not a legitimate one, although a lot of its members are high up in the bureaucracy and elective offices. Long before they become such a respected public entity, I had a run-in with one of their cells.

"In Washington. They were plotting to assassinate the president and put their own man in his place. Their goal, then and now, is world domination.

"Cottler knew about that and intended to expose the whole thing. He was murdered for the information he had, and the only materials destroyed referred to the planned shows on the SIE. A sloppy job, at that. Whoever did it failed to take or damage other data to throw investigators off the trail. They even left the text of one show on an IBM memory typewriter. It shows a dull single-mindedness that makes me think of one of the lower-grade Communist intelligence agencies—the Vietnamese, or North Korea, or perhaps Cuba."

"I can't imagine a man like David Felder, a philanthropist, a confidant of presidents and kings, who is so concerned with social justice, being part of an—an international conspiracy."

The Penetrator smiled to soften his words. "Don't let yourself be misled by a well-planned puff job by the media. Most of the major newspapers, the networks, many influential magazines, are now owned or controlled by Felder or other members of the SIE. It's easy to look good if you are your own PR agency."

"It sounds grotesque, Machiavellian."

"All the same it's true. These children who are missing. Are all of them boys?"

"No. Out of the four institutions, five of them are girls."

Mark paused with his sandwich half way to his mouth. He shook his head in frustration. "That makes even less sense than what I had before. Yet, there must be some connection. The SIE, the Felder Foundation, Cottler's murder, the orphanages, and your missing kids. Somewhere there's a connection." Mark abruptly changed the subject, smiled at Angie with boyish engagement.

"But that'll come later. Let's talk about you and me. How about a date tonight, gorgeous?"

"Yes, darling. I've been wondering when you'd ask. Dinner at my place? I have a new condo, really super. Then dancing, if we can find a place owned by one of our fellow non-Mormons."

"Fine with me. Seven o'clock be okay?"

"Come at six and I'll fix you a drink."

"You're on."

# 7

## INTERRUPTED PLANS

Mark Hardin rang the doorbell below the large, brass number 23 on Angie's English-country-manor-style, two-story condominium at ten minutes of six. Immediately high-pitched, yelling voices and the thunderous sound of rushing footsteps descending a staircase came from inside. The lowering sun sent orange glints off the gently rocking surface of the large swimming pool that dominated the center of the complex. The door flew open to reveal Kevin and Karen, Angie's twins.

"Hi, Mark," they chorused. "C'mon in." They were both barefoot and wore wet swimsuits. They flashed identical, silvery, brace-banded smiles. The recent summer had tanned their bodies a healthy glowing, deep iced-tea brown which contrasted nicely with their cottony off-white hair and dark azure eyes.

"You shoulda come earlier and taken a swim with us," Kevin admonished.

The Penetrator entered and closed the door behind him. "The name's Miller this time. Greg Miller."

*Penetrator work again.* Kevin and Karen exchanged a silent communication in that special manner common to many twins.

A pink stain rose from the low top of Kevin's skimpy racing trunks until the embarrassment he felt flushed his face. "I'm sorry. Mom told us, but I forgot."

"All right, this time, Tiger. But \ 'ch it."

Angie entered the living room then in time to save her son's discomfort. Arms open, she crossed to Mark and embraced him, planting warm, soft lips on his in a passionate kiss.

"Welcome home, guy," she murmured when their greeting ended. Then she looked at her children. "You two! Water rats, that's what you are. I can't keep them out of the pool," she explained to Mark.

"It's an indoor-outdoor arrangement so the kids can swim all year. Honestly, it's a battle to get them out and send them off to school."

"And we have a sauna and whirlpool too," Karen informed the Penetrator.

"We have our own hot tub out on the patio," Kevin added. "I like it better. Kar and me were on our way when you rang. Wanna share?"

Long accustomed to the casual personal attitudes within the privacy of the Dillon household, the Penetrator smiled with a warmth that nearly displayed parental affection and pride. "Sure. Why not? Are you going in?" he asked Angie.

"I—well, no. My dinner. It'll—oh, all right. I'm a sucker for that sybaritic tub."

"Great! You can undress in my room," Kevin offered Mark.

"No," Karen corrected her brother, woman-wise for her twelve years. "In Mom's."

"Okay," Kevin agreed, unaffected by the change. "I'll get you a towel, Mark—uh, Greg."

"Good boy."

Karen escorted the Penetrator upstairs to the large master bedroom and left him there. He removed his clothes and accepted a large, nubbily soft towel from Kevin, who now wore a similar one wrapped around his waist. The three of them went downstairs together.

Out on the patio, in the chill early fall air, thick tendrils of steam rose from the dark surface six inches below the rim of a huge hot tub that looked like half of a wine fermenting vat. The youngsters threw off their brightly colored coverings and leaped into the seething water. Mark followed at a slower pace, retrieving their abandoned towels and hanging them on pegs alongside his own. Naked, he eased himself into the invigorating bath.

Instantly he was overwhelmed by two wriggling, bare young bodies. Laughing and splashing, the twins ducked Mark under the vaporous surface. Angie joined them in a few minutes, a vision in a hip-length terry-cloth robe. On a tray she carried Pepsis in insulated can holders for Kevin and Karen and two gigantic *piña coladas* for herself and Mark in large, thermal plastic containers fashioned to look like coconut shells.

She distributed the drinks and removed her wrapper. Then she slipped her firm, lusciously tanned nude body into the welcoming water.

"Hummmm. See what I mean about sybaritic?" she murmured close to the Penetrator's ear.

"Love it. I absolutely love it."

Dinner, a masterpiece of beef in oyster sauce, shrimp, egg foo yong, rice, and almond duck in plum sauce, didn't get served until seven-thirty. Seated around a warmly homey table in the dinette, they filled each other in on their lives since last they had been together and latest letters had been sent both directions. The twins were allowed two small cups each of hot sake and relished their last one slowly while Angie rose to refresh Mark's tiny porcelain container and bring the fortune cookies.

"Ummmm," she began once more in her chair. "A little bad news, I'm afraid." She glanced at the children. "Though we shouldn't discuss it here."

"What is it, Angie?"

"When I got back to my office, we had received confirmation on those questionable orphanages. Three children no longer are present in each of two institutions we had on the suspected list. That makes a total of thirty-five in the state."

"What are the names of the institutions?"

"Glenn Ivy Youth Center and the Merritt Children's Center."

"Both private operations and both on the list of those receiving funding from the Felder Foundation. Thirty-five for Utah. Imagine what that could amount to if this were nationwide. Damnit, Angie, there has to be a connection, though I can't figure out what it is. Why would they want children? For what? How old are the missing ones?"

"All between twelve and seventeen."

"White slavery? If so, why pick people on whom records exist?"

"Let it go," Angie advised. "Time enough for that tomorrow."

When the last crisp rice-flour fortune cookie had been opened, its message read and laughed over, and the sweet shell consumed, Angie rose and tousled the soft blond hair of her pug-nosed, freckled look-alikes. "Homework for an hour and a half, no more. Then off to bed. No television, it's a week night. We'll be home about midnight."

"Okay, Mom," they answered together, rising to clear the clutter of dishes from the table. The wires and metal caps of their braces glittered in the candlelight.

At a quarter past twelve, Mark looked in on the youngsters. Both had kicked off their covers. They lay on their bellies, sleeping soundly, neither wearing pajama tops. Mark drew the sheet and light blanket up around Karen's shoulders, feeling strangely soft and sentimental while he did. Then he went to Kevin's room and repeated the process.

Back in the master bedroom, Mark began to unbutton his shirt. Angie, naked and glowing, lithely crossed the room to him and placed a warm, silky hand on his bronze, bare chest.

"Oh, wow! That terrific bod of yours got me all weak, moist, and squirmy out there in the hot tub. I could hardly keep my hands off you."

"I know," the Penetrator murmured. "It was all I could do to keep from rising to the occasion."

"A good thing you did. The kids know we sleep together and, somehow, I don't mind that. But—right then and there—it could have been a heavy scene."

"Public displays aren't my long suit either."
Mark slid out of his trousers and undershorts, his tu-
mescent organ thrust hungrily toward Angie's
eager body. "Now we're alone . . ." he kissed her.
"With no one . . ." again their lips met. "To disturb
. . ." their tongues flirted yet another time in their
open mouths. "Us."

Angie trembled at the rigid pressure of Mark's
maleness against her firm, flat abdomen and her
reply came as a moan of exquisite delight, mingled with the depthless agony of loneliness. "Oh,
now. Take me now, Mark, like you used to. I-I want
you so much. Please, please, do it now. Hurry!"

Mark lifted Angie and carried her to the bed. He
put her down gently and entered her vibratingly
ready body slowly, prolonging the giddy mad-
ness that engulfed them both, while he sinuously
drove the thick bulk and silken length of his burn-
ing shaft deeper. With a final thrust, they joined,
soul to soul.

The magnitude of his piercing popped open
Angie's eyes. Glazed and unfocused, they tried to
study his face, pressed so close to her own. "Oh,
yes. Yes! That's it! That's how I want it. Oh, yes.
More! More!"

Mark began to move in a languid rhythm that
quickly took them beyond the veil of reality, so
that fragile mortality itself lost meaning and
ceased to threaten them with each tick of the cosmic clock. The eternal NOW seized them and
made them one.

A long, loving time later they lay at peace. Their
bodies curved together, spoon-fashion, Mark
held Angie to him and gently caressed one of her
full, up-tilted breasts. He felt an answering surge in

his loins when the dark nipple grew erect with renewed desire.

"Ummmmh. This is how I want it to be—always," Angie muttered softly."

"It could be . . ." Mark left it open.

"M-Mark? Are—are you proposing marriage to me?"

Mark found himself stammering like a nervous teenager. "I—well, I—Oh, God, Angie. I don't know what I mean. Only—that I love you so much."

"We're good together, you know that? I don't mean just the sex thing. We're—really—good together. We think alike about right and wrong, about how kids should be raised and in what kind of world. And it's not too late, you know—to raise another family, I mean."

"The twins are growing up," Mark observed with caution.

"Sure. Kids do that. They can be a big help with little brothers and sisters."

"I don't mean that way alone. How do I say this? They're—ah, postpubescent now."

"Don't I know it! Karen's gonna have a set of knockers that will make me jealous."

"That's what I'm talking about. I got some rather long and searching looks from Karen out there at the hot tub and not in what you could call a daughterly fashion."

"So? She's been ogling her brother that way since they've both begun to develop. Speaking of which, Kevin, now that he's started to feel his oats, needs a father's influence more than ever. Yet, I don't see incest rearing its ugly head in this family.

Even with some new additions, starting with you, darling."

"How can you be so sure that the changes they're experiencing won't affect them in a way, once we became a permanant thing, that will shatter the closeness we four have now?"

"Oh, pooh, darling. I'm the teacher, remember, all crammed full of child development and psych courses. In this instance, Mother really does know best. The kids love you, worship you, truth to tell. No ugly ogre of a stepfather for them. Now turn me around and make love to me again and let these weighty matters take care of themselves."

This time the Penetrator turned out the light.

Two-thirty in the morning came and the Penetrator's automatic mental alarm awakened him. He quickly dressed and left Angie's condo. His destination: the Carstairs Foundling Home.

This was to be a soft probe, so the Penetrator had brought along only Ava, set of lockpicks, and a flashlight. As an afterthought he took his electronic safe-cracking amplifier. He drove slowly past the Carstairs home and parked half a block away. He returned on silent, moccasined feet to check the perimeter fence and gate.

He saw no sign of anyone on the playground, nor on the small swatch of lawn in front of the main entrance. The gate, open during the day, now stood closed and locked, with a night watchman in a small box to one side. The Penetrator slid Ava from its shoulder holster and openly approached the barrier. Immediately the guard came from his post to check.

Mark shot him from a distance of twenty feet. The sleeper dart dropped the man before he could cry out. The Penetrator quickly closed the distance and inserted pick and tension bar into the keyway of the lock on a small personnel gate inset into the larger grillwork. Two short seconds and he had it open. Mark glanced down at the unconscious sentry and noted he was an Oriental. Also that he was armed with a handgun. Armed guards for an orphanage? His hunch grew nearer to a certainty. In short rush he covered the distance to the building front.

The moon came out from behind high, scudding clouds and for a moment froze the Penetrator in place. Then he eased his way toward the shadow side of the orphanage and located a side entrance he'd made note of earlier. Once again he resorted to lockpicks. This time it took him a bit longer. A tough Segal lock inset in the metal-covered door made slow going. At last it clicked and the Penetrator slipped inside and closed it behind him.

Mark quickly oriented himself in the hallway and headed toward Meeks's office. It was there, he believed, he would find what he needed. Another locked door. The excessive security only fueled his suspicions. The Penetrator manipulated the bolt, entered, and made his way to a file cabinet. *Here a lock, there a lock,* the Penetrator thought with irritation, *everywhere a . . .* another set of tumblers yielded to his efforts and he opened the first drawer.

Dossiers on the children. All conveniently arranged in alphabetical order. Quickly the

Penetrator went through the files, seeking the names provided by Angie of the youngsters supposedly missing. Not a single folder remained for any of them. Mark did find a file on a boy named Dennis Roberts and, from the lad's photograph, identified him as the blond kid who had given him silent, smiling approval of his opinion of the oddball history lesson. With boys like that, he thought, and Angie's twins, growing up in the country, some hope remained. He went through the other drawers without result, then turned to Meeks's desk.

Another blank, the Penetrator quickly found out. Not a scrap of information presented itself that would explain SIE's involvement with orphaned children. Though he did spot bus schedules for Greyhound and Continental Trailways from Salt Lake to Seattle, for whatever that might mean. Then, in a hidden lockbox, he located a stack of Polaroid shots.

Disgust rose in the Penetrator's throat while he went through the photographs. Graphic, sexually explicit porno nudie poses by boys and girls he recognized as residents of the foundling home, none of them over thirteen, some of the scenes including Meeks himself, filled the metal container. Could he have been right about a white-slave ring? He promptly rejected the idea. Not a big enough profit in it for SIE. This had to be a private, personal kink of Arnold Meeks. The Penetrator silently promised to pay back the slimy bastard if he got the chance. He returned the perverse collection to its hiding place and closed Meeks's desk. Not much for his efforts. Resignedly he made a final check to be sure everything remained as it had been before, then crossed to the hallway door.

A grunt of effort warned the Penetrator in time to dart the man who attacked him from the left. The security guard went into convulsions before his agonized body hit the floor.

A voice on Mark's right called out in a singsong language.

Although he didn't recognize the words, they could have been Manchurian or Korean, the Penetrator thought when the man spoke again. The order not to move or else had a universality about it that made the meaning clear. Mark tensed himself and made as though to comply.

Mark's low, sweeping kick that caught the man at his ankles and cleaned him off his feet came as a big surprise. The brief pain in his chest from the $CO_2$-powered dart completed the security man's astonishment a moment before he twitched and jerked into unconsciousness. The Penetrator ran to the side door and slipped out into the night.

The time had come. Dennis Roberts had made careful plans. He had confided in Devon and Wes that he intended to run away from the orphanage. Even if winter was coming, he could hide out in some big city where it stayed nice, like L.A. or Miami, keep away from the cops and he'd be okay. After a while, he felt sure, they would all stop looking for him and he could openly go anywhere he wanted. He'd get a job, maybe running one of those corner newsstands like he'd seen in movies about New York City. He could easily pass for thirteen. In his boyish enthusiasm, Dennis had completely overlooked the fact that his short stature and slenderness, despite his stocky, muscular shoulders and legs, made him look more like ten than thirteen. No matter, he wasn't going to stay and let that old fart DiFalco preach all that Commie crap at him.

He knew better. His dad and mom had taught him about loving his country and being proud to be an American. And that weirdo Meeks, always rubbin' and pattin' his bare butt before applying the strap. Queer-o! No more of that where he was going. Dennis tied together his small bundle of possessions and opened the door to his room.

He silently ran on bare tiptoes to the end of the hallway, his sneakers clutched in one hand. His luck held and he made it to the ground floor without being seen. He knew his buddies would cover for him, not squeal or anything, until he had a chance to get a long ways away from this rotten place. He nearly blundered into the lower corridor, though, before he spotted Chiun and Ong approaching quietly in their silly-looking silk slippers.

They stopped at either side of the doorway to Meeks's office. Dennis crouched low and peeked around the baseboard at the stair entrance. He hardly dared to breathe for fear the two goons would discover him. Even his heartbeat seemed loud in his own ears. Could they hear it? Then the door opened and someone dressed all in dark clothes came out.

With a start, Dennis recognized the big, black-haired guy who had visited their class that morning. The one who had made the neat-o crack about DiFalco and his love for Fidel Castro. He'd sounded angry, too. He must be some kind of spy, Dennis decided. Gonna get the goods on Meeks, DiFalco, and company for the CIA. Love it! Dennis rejoiced silently. Then Ong attacked the intruder. Dennis wanted to cry a warning, but he was suddenly scared of what might happen to him.

He heard a soft hiss, like escaping gas, a moment before fat Ong went down and started flopping around the floor like a fish out of water. Far out, Dennis exulted.

Chiun grunted something in his gook language and the tough-lookin' guy kicked Chiun's feet out from under him and shot him, too. Was that what a silencer sounded like, Dennis wondered. Chiun dropped to the floor and began to twitch. Then the big dude ran right past where Dennis hid and let himself out the side door.

All hell would break loose, and fast, Dennis reasoned. His chance of making an escape were slim and none. Reluctantly he started back up the stairs toward his lonely and imprisoning room. At least, he rationalized, he'd seen a couple of those nerds get what was good for them. He could escape another time. Maybe the counter-spy would come back; he could ask to go along then. He knew a lot about Carstairs Foundling Home that the FBI or whoever would probably love to know. Dennis had, without realizing it, acquired a hero, someone to give him hope.

Yeah. That's what he'd do. He'd watch and when the superspook came back, he'd reveal his knowledge and escape with the help of the CIA. That'd really make Meeks and the rest pay.

# 8

## "LETS'S HELP MARK"

"Well—what do you think, Kar?" Kevin Dillon anxiously asked his sister.

"I don't know, Kevie. What good will it do?"

"You heard what Mark said at breakfast. He didn't find out anything he wanted to know. Today's Friday, then two days of no school. We can do it easy, huh? Can't we, huh?"

"How do you expect to get away with it?"

"Simple. When we come home this afternoon, we change, go over there and—just mix in."

"Brilliant plan, brother dear. What if we get caught? Or worse still, what if they think we really do belong there and we never get out?"

"Don't worry, Kar. Nothin's going to happen. Trust me."

Karen frowned. "That's what Jimmy Carter said."

Karen Dillon dropped from the monkey bars on the playground of the Carstairs Foundling Home, her eyes wide with worry. "Oh-oh, Kevie. Here comes one of them. I—I'm scared."

"Don't worry, Sis. He's just another kid."

"Hi, I'm Dennis. You two are new here, aren't you?"

The three youngsters looked remarkably alike, with their pale blond hair, dark-colored eyes, and light dustings of freckles. They stood of a height, give or take an inch. Karen remained speechless, but Kevin quickly took the initiative, after a brief nibble at one fingernail.

"Uh—yeah. We just came in this afternoon. I'm Kevin and this is my sister, Karen. We're twins."

"I noticed," Dennis responded dryly. "I've never seen you around before, that's why I figured you were new. In fact," Dennis's eyes glowed with a shrewd light. "You kids don't really belong here, do you?"

"Oooh, Kevie, I told you so."

Kevin started to protest, but Dennis cut him off. "Hey, I don't really care. What I can't understand is why. When everyone here would give his arm to get out, what made you want to come in?"

"Uh—I don't know. We only wanted to look around, I guess," Kevin replied. Such searching questions from a kid no older than himself put him off balance. "What tipped you off?"

Dennis pointed to the clothes worn by Kevin and Karen, matched pairs of Ocean Pacific shorts, pullover shirts and Adidas runners. "They don't buy expensive clothes like that for kids in here. And they can't afford braces for those who need them either. I don't buy this, 'We just wanted to look around,' either. Look, Kev, you gotta have a reason," Dennis admonished. "What is it? Tell me."

Kevin looked down at his blue Adidas runners, scuffed at the sand of the playground. Karen's eyes filled with tears. All around them the sounds of children at play filled the air. Dennis likewise hesitated. His high intelligence gave him an ability to quickly analyze situations and understand people.

"Uh, listen, Kev, I'm on punishment. I'm not even supposed to be out here right now. So I'm as much in the wrong as you two. I'll help you, but I gotta know what's going on."

"We—we're helping a friend."

Excitement and hope fired up in Dennis. He flashed small, even white teeth behind an engaging smile. "You mean someone inside here? Are you plannin' a breakout?"

"No—not exactly that. Some funny things are supposed to be going on around here," Kevin explained. "Our friend tried to find out about 'em last night and didn't learn anything. He also got jumped by some Jap guards."

"They aren't Japanese," Dennis corrected automatically. "They're Korean. North Korean, I think." Suddenly the realization of what Kevin had said struck him. "You mean—the spy? You are working for *him?*" Dennis bent over and repeatedly slapped his bare right thigh. All the while he gleefully shouted, "I love it! You're working for the CIA. Are you midgets?" He studied Kevin and Karen with critical appraisal. "Naw. You're real kids, all right."

"He's not a spy and he's not from the CIA," Karen interrupted indignantly. "He's the—"

"Shut up, Karen!" Kevin commanded. "We—

we're not exactly working for him. He doesn't know we're here."

Dennis sobered. "Then you're in some deep stuff. Oh-oh, here comes old Blubber Bottom."

"Who?"

"Mrs. Durfee, the playground supervisor. If she finds us together, we're all in the soup. C'mon. I'll hide you out until later."

The three youngsters ran across the open field and entered the main building. The composition soles of their runners slapped loudly on the highly polished rubber tiles of the hallway. Dennis pointed to one doorway.

"In there, Karen."

"I don't have to go to the bathroom."

"Do it. Sit in one of the stalls and keep your head down. Nobody will bother you that way." He led Kevin next door to the boys' room. Dennis felt satisfied when Kevin darted toward the swinging door without the need of further explanations.

"I'll come back for you as soon as I can. Now I've got to get my room before Blubber Bottom catches me and I really get it."

"What's your room number—just in case?"

"Good thinkin', Kev. Two-oh-seven. Upstairs at the far end of the hall. Hang loose."

"For sure," Kevin responded fervently.

Angie Dillon returned from work at five that afternoon. Funny, she thought when she entered the living room of her condo, no good smells coming from the casserole she'd instructed Karen to put in the oven. If she'd gone off to the pool, without tending to her chores, there was one young lady who would hear about it, but good. Angie crossed to the dining area and the folded piece of composition paper immediately caught her attention. She picked it up and rapidly scanned the scrawly lines of her son's wretched handwriting.

"Dear Mom, Karen and me have gone to help Mark. No one will suspect kids in an orphanage, right? So don't worry about us and we'll be back no later than Sunday with some information. Love ya, Kevin."

A premonition of impending disaster sent a chill over Angie's body and she shook herself. Funny, she thought absently, at a time like this her mind resorted to clichés. Yet, the chill was real enough and she did fear for her children. Oh, when would Mark get back? What could he do?

Half an hour later, the Penetrator arrived. He quickly set the bundles he carried on the large, hatch-cover cocktail table when he saw the stricken look on Angie's face.

"What happened?"

"Kevin and Karen have gone over to that orphanage. They got in their heads somehow that they can help you that way. Oh, God, Mark, if what you say is true, they're in terrible danger."

"Take it easy, sweetheart. I'll go after them, of course. It will take a little planning, but don't worry. I'll have them back here before anything can go wrong."

The ground floor of the Carstairs Foundling Home was off limits following the evening meal. The offices and rest-rooms lay in darkness, relieved only slightly by the single bulbs glowing at each end of the hallway. Dennis Roberts moved cautiously down the corridor and slipped into the boys' room. To give himself a quasi-legitimate reason for being there in the event of discovery, he popped open the front of his short trousers and urinated into the troughlike fixture attached to one wall. Over the splashing of his relief call, Dennis harshly whispered.

"Kevin—you still there?"

"Of course I am," came Kevin's reply from inside one closed stall. "Where else would I be?"

"Good. Go get your sister and we'll hit old man Meeks's office."

"Uh—okay—but, I gotta go too. I was afraid to move or make any noise until you came back."

"All right. I'll finish up and go do it. Hurry, though."

Five minutes later the three youngsters crouched at the door to Arnold Meeks's office. Dennis diligently worked on the lock with a pair of unbent paper clips. The tumblers reluctantly retreated into line and the door latch clicked open.

The children tumbled inside. "Wow!" Kevin enthused in admiration. "Where'd you learn to do that?"

"I was in a foster home for a couple of months right after my folks were killed and the cops looked for some relatives. It turned out that the old guy that took me in was a retired burglar. He taught me all sorts of neat tricks before his wife got on him about it."

"For sure, Dennis. For sure." Kevin turned on a desk lamp.

"Now, old Meeks has all sorts of secret ways to hide stuff he don't want people to see. One day when I was in here to get my butt whipped, I saw him put away a file on our special classes under 'Plumbing Blueprints' in that cabinet over there."

"Did you really get whippings?" Karen asked timidly.

"Sure. With that strap hanging right up there."

Kevin and Karen stared in open-mouthed awe at the instrument of punishment. They'd both been spanked with their mother's bare hand and had privileges suspended as punishment, but the thought of being whaled upon with a leather paddle filled them with dread.

Kevin turned his attention to the file cabinet. "Hey, this thing is locked."

"Let me at it, then," Dennis advised. In thirty seconds he had the lock released. "There, nothin' simpler."

Karen found the plumbing-blueprint file. The two boys gathered around her. "Look at this. Far out! 'Order of Battle for Juvenile Irregulars.' What the heck is that? And this one, 'Invasion Scenario for the DMZ.' Cripers, is Meeks planning a war?"

"Oh, that crap," Dennis dismissed the papers. "They make us play war games out in the desert during summer. FTX's they call 'em. We throw dummy grenades, carry knives and machetes, all that sort of stuff. I think it's just some wild idea dreamed up by Meeks and DiFalco. They're both a couple of nuts. An' that old bitch, Durfee, is just as crazy. She runs around in uniform, yellin' orders an' such. Dumb," Dennis summed it up.

"Ma—uh, Greg will sure want to see this," Karen advised them.

"There's more stuff, I'm sure. But I can't crack a safe," Dennis informed them.

"And you won't get the chance, you little monster," Arnold Meeks thundered from the open doorway.

"Oh, *shit,*" Dennis gasped, completely unmindful of his language in front of adults in the shock of being caught.

"Me too," Kevin groaned.

Meeks and three Orientals entered. The foundling home's director stalked directly to Dennis and clapped a hard hand on his shoulder, thumb pressing into the youngster's throat. He began violently to shake the boy.

"You goddamned little sneak. I should have taken care of you a long time ago. Go get Dr. DiFalco," Meeks ordered one of the Koreans. Three minutes later the graying teacher entered the office.

"What's going on here?" he demanded.

"See what your pleas for leniency got us? I don't care if you are some sort of power in SIE and I'm supposed to do as you say. I told you we should have terminated this little bastard a month ago."

"Watch that loose mouth of yours, Meeks," DiFalco snapped. "Who are these other children?"

"How should I know? They're with him and they've gotten into the files. All three of them have to die now."

Karen began to cry, great, silent tears running down her lightly tanned cheeks. Kevin put a protective arm around his sister's shoulders and scowled at Meeks.

"You son of a bitch," Kevin enunciated slowly and clearly, each word coated with venom.

Meeks struck with blind ferocity. His hand left a livid mark on Kevin's cheek. "Take them out and kill them," Meeks instructed the Korean guards. "Bury the bodies in the desert."

Before the three men could move, the door crashed open.

The Penetrator stood in the opening, his Star PD, .45 pistol in his right hand and Ava, his silent, deadly dart gun fisted in the left. Ava hissed, tracked, and hissed a second time.

Chiun and one of the other guards crashed to the floor, fatally injected with curarine. The remaining Korean drew his sidearm, an aged Radom 9mm with a loose slide. Meeks struggled to free a .25 automatic from his coat pocket.

Too many targets, the Penetrator thought in haste, and the kids in the way too. "Get down!" he roared at them in the full force of his command voice.

Kevin, Karen, and Dennis obeyed instantly. They dived out of sight behind Meeks's desk. Mark swung his PD onto the security type and squeezed the trigger.

The Star emitted a deafening roar in the confines of the office. The bullet smacked into shoulder flesh, partly turning the Korean.

Ong, the remaining Korean intelligence agent, although wounded, pumped a shot at his sudden attacker. The slug missed and struck a large loving cup on a bookshelf with a resounding clang. The trophy rocked, spun, and fell to the floor. Ong didn't have time to correct his aim.

The Penetrator's second round boomed into the gunpowder-smelling office. Ong developed a third, sightless, eye where his nose had been and he slammed backward into the open file cabinet. Amid a resounding clatter of metal he crashed to the floor. Arnold Meeks had produced his own firearm and the diminutive pistol fired with its characteristic nasty, toy-poodle snarl.

Meeks's first shot sent a copper-jacketed pellet wide of the Penetrator's head by a safe foot. The second one cut cloth in Mark's jacket and burned a painful streak across his left shoulder. The third one would have struck the Penetrator in the heart had not Dennis hit the foundling-home director in the back of the head with a well-thrown book. By then, Mark had the Star PD trained on his tormentor.

Two .45 JHP expanders popped into the bone structure of Meeks's face and exploded out the back of his head. Blood, brain matter, bone chips, and spinal fluid spewed out over the desk and wall behind. Some of it splashed on Dennis's face.

The boy, so filled with battle fire a second earlier, lost the color from his sagging features, his complexion drained a pale, green-white. Dennis bent to one side and retched violently. The remains of his supper gushed out onto the floor and he dropped into the sheltering protection of the desk, beside Kevin and Karen.

Dr. Treavor DiFalco rushed the Penetrator, not in a desire to fight, but to escape. He knew his own importance to the overall project and he had no desire to remain and die alongside a bungler like Arnold Meeks. His charge momentarily knocked the Penetrator off balance. The two men grappled a second, then DiFalco broke free and ran down the hallway. Mark turned his attention back to the room.

"Come on, you two. Let's get out of here. Kevin—Karen?" he called again.

Two blond heads appeared above the desk top, cobalt eyes wide with fear. "Dennis has gotta come too," Kevin demanded.

"I haven't time to argue. I came here to keep you out of trouble. There's bound to be more guards. *Let's go!*"

"Not without Dennis," Karen replied defiantly. "He—he saved your life. They'll kill him if you don't let him come."

Oh, hell, Mark thought, what would he do with an escaped orphan on his hands? The kids were right, though. The boy's life would be in danger if left behind. "All right. Hurry."

A burst of automatic-weapon fire rattled from down the hallway. The Penetrator barely managed to jerk the children back inside the office before the slugs chewed the doorframe to kindling. Damn. If only he hadn't left the Sidewinder behind. Mark dug into one coat pocket and came out with a small piece of C-4 plastic explosive. Risky, but how else could he be sure of silencing the chopper and giving them a halfway even chance to escape?"

The Penetrator removed the powerful substance from the sandwich bag he'd carried it in, unwrapped the plastic film covering it, and squeezed it around a small time-pencil detonator. He set the device for thirty seconds, the shortest delay possible, then hazarded a quick glance out the door.

A sudden splatter of bullets trashed a display case to one side of the office. Mark returned fire and then hurled the explosive down the hallway in a sidearm pitch. It hit, skidded into a pool of darkness, and lay in the open. The submachine gun chattered again and a man darted out to try to retrieve the deadly object. The Penetrator shot his legs out from under him.

Then the blast went off.

Lights winked out, their globes shattered by the concussion, which also broke windows and display-case fronts and started two doors afire. That immediately set off the sprinkler system. The Penetrator changed magazines and emptied the new one down the hallway. Mark gathered the children together, put a fresh load in the Star PD, and gave the youngsters terse instructions.

"Keep low, run like hell, and head for the side door."

The Penetrator came out last, in a crouch. He fired at random down the corridor and ran backward. Seconds passed before he joined Kevin, Karen, and Dennis outside. Then the beleaguered quartet darted wildly across the front lawn, toward the open gate and safety.

# 9

## SIE CONQUEST

"You mean to tell me that you abandoned the entire operation at the Carstairs place because of one man?" David Felder angrily paced the floor of his huge ski lodge in Aspen, Colorado. He stopped, unable even to stride away his fury when Doctor DiFaclo began his reply.

"Yes sir. We had no choice. The explosions, fire, gun shots in the night, and the dead and wounded. When the police came, well—naturally they took the children. Durfee and I barely managed to get away. I'm certain, though, that the man involved was the Penetrator. Why, he—he even had some youngsters working with him."

"*That* surprises you?" David Felder riposted acidly. "Particularly considering your role in this project? Now listen to me, *Dr.* DiFalco. This is big, doctor. The biggest effort the SIE has launched since that—ah, tragic reversal we experienced a few years ago. Let me refresh your memory, in the event it failed to properly impress you before.

"We are going to mastermind another brushfire war. A full-scale shoot-'em-up that will, hopefully, so thoroughly demoralize this country's armed forces, and the civilian population, that they will never again resort to arms. Will, in fact, not even fight to defend their homeland. Then we move in and take over without firing a shot." Pleased with the enormity of his grand design, Felder walked to the small bar in one corner, poured himself a steaming cup of coffee, and laced it with Kaluha.

Yes, a magnificent plan, Felder thought. He had sold it to the ruling inner circle of the society, and the reward for its success had been his conception also. Think of it! Absolute master over 200 million stupid, but tractable, slaves. David Felder, corporate director of what used to be the United States of America. Power. Power to control every aspect of the lives and deaths of those servants of the Corporate Godhead. Crushing taxes for the masses to keep them in their proper places while we of the elite, the Chosen, revel in unbelievable luxury, unknown since the days of Nero. His thoughts mellowed his raging mood. He sipped appreciatively of his liqueur-laced coffee and returned to tower over the chair in which Dr. Treavor DiFalco slumped in dejection. He forced his voice to take on a reasoning tone, as though lecturing at a board of director's meeting in the bank.

"The secret alliance between the society and the People's Republic of North Korea is the lever we will use to precipitate this war. When South Korea is invaded, the United States will, naturally, come to the aid of their ally. In addition to the enormous profits we can expect to make in our individually owned companies that hold Defense Department contracts—like we did during Vietnam—we will unleash a form of terrorist warfare, and stage a huge media event covering it, that should guarantee a wave of antigovernment and antimilitary sentiment that can result in toppling the current administration, and this time, with it, that despicable Constitution that prevents us from doing as we wish.

"American and South Korean troops will be forced to fire in self-defense and world opinion will do the rest. And your part in all this, doctor, is the very keystone of our success." Felder paused again, sipped from his mug.

"You are supposed to supervise the behavior modification and indoctrination of these little monsters in your charge. These children must become highly motivated so that when the time comes for them to pour down over the thirty-eighth parallel into South Korea with knives, guns, and hand grenades—which they will use on U.S. troops while they stand around in sweet-faced innocence begging for chocolate or food—it can be accomplished without hesitation. The more brutish of your charges are to be used as an assault force to support the little assassins, as you well know. With the exception of a few hundred, the main force is not yet capable of performing their assignment. How can this be accomplished if our training schools are closed down?"

"I—well, sir, the Carstairs home was only one of many. We can still fill the quota. Time isn't that critical a factor, is it? If I am assured of your assistance and the cooperation of these gentlemen, I can still bring it off." Treavor DiFalco ran nervous fingers through the graying hair at one temple and looked with appeal at the other men in the room.

Colonel Kum Lok Gee, head of the North Korean

intelligence liaison team, stared impassively
back at Dr. DiFalco. How stupid and frenetic are
these Occidentals, he thought to himself. Any
competent person knew that it took years to properly indoctrinate and motivate subjects for this sort
of suicide mission. Yet, the children would prove a
useful diversion. Then, once they had consoli-
dated achievements of their invasion of the South
and that cursed Park's government collapsed,
the People's Republic of Korea, as a unified country, would be more than in position to dictate
terms to these upstarts. The *Société Internationale
d'Élite.* As though any Occidental could aspire to
elite status. Five thousand years of Oriental civili-
zation mocked that absurdity.

First the South, then Japan. Who knows? With the
backing of the government in Peking, they might
even expand to the Philippines. This vain little
Western creature wanted cooperation. Well and
good. He'd get it, though only in the form of increased security at the other training facilities.
Gee barely inclined his leonine head in a sign of
acknowledgement. His whipcord-spare frame
and hard-lined face revealed the disciplined
body and mind of a professional soldier, despite
his mufti.

"Thank you, Colonel Gee," DiFalco breathed
with relief. Nearly three hundred juveniles had
been gathered at the safe house on the West
Coast. Without Gee's full cooperation, how could
a force that size be kept under control? His gaze
passed on to Gore Sasson. DiFalco didn't like the
pudgy little French-Canadian. A *séparatist*, at
times he seemed more dedicated to the cause of
Quebec separatism than to the SIE. Now Sasson

wet thick, overred lips and steepled his thick, short fingers.

"Am I to assume that we three will still be required to journey to North Korea during the final stage of preparing these youngsters?"

"Yes," David Felder replied. "And the time for that grows a lot closer than you originally supposed. Within less than a week the first contingent of youngsters is to depart from our safe house on the West Coast for North Korea." The assembled men exchanged looks of consternation. "The entire timetable has been accelerated because of the current administration.

"If it weren't for the man in power now, we wouldn't even need this bizarre diversion. It had already been arranged to pull American troops out of South Korea and thus pave the way for an invasion from the North. The assassination of Sadat, and the resultant unrest in the Middle East, has kept everyone's attention focused in the wrong direction for quite some time. Yet, because of the present climate in this country, we must employ devious means. Not only have we lost control over the White House, but a number of valuable seats in the Senate and House. The people remain solidly behind this change in political climate, and the best intelligence reports indicate that the North Korean forces haven't a chance of success without assistance." David Felder looked to Colonel Gee for verification.

"Quite right, Mr. Felder. Without some means of creating a wave of revulsion that will disaffect the people of your country, why, I'm afraid your army might go in there and actually win. Then, where would we all be?"

"Where indeed." Felder needn't remind them more of past defeats. "So, Dr. DiFalco, instead of biding your time, you must speed up the process. Use more subliminals on the television, use narcotics if necessary. You can no longer afford the luxury of commanding your kiddie army from one central headquarters. You must get out there and make personal contact and see to it that the shipments of children are ready on demand."

"I—" Treavor DiFalco hesitated only a fraction of a second. "I'll see that it is done. But, what about the Penetrator?"

"Let me worry about him. I can guarantee you that a week from now," David Felder paused in satisfied contemplation of his revelation, "he won't even be alive."

While Treavor DiFalco attended his heated, early-morning conference in Aspen, the Penetrator summoned three sleepy-eyed youngsters from their beds for a debriefing. Dennis had bunked in with Kevin and the two boys scrambled downstairs together. Dennis bubbled over with excitement when he entered the living room.

"Boy! I still can't get over it. Being rescued by the CIA. Super."

"I don't work for the CIA, Dennis," the Penetrator told him.

"The FBI, then, huh?"

"Nope."

"Then—what? Who are you?"

"He's the Penetra . . ." Karen started to say from the stair landing. She clapped three fingers over her mouth and her eyes went wide in deep blue consternation. "Ooops! I wasn't supposed to tell that."

"The *Penetrator*?" Dennis's voice rose a squeaky half-octave. "You mean I'm sitting beside the—the Penetrator and you're—you're *for real*?"

Mark Hardin looked embarrassed, which masked the enormous concern he felt for the child's safety. "I'm afraid so, Dennis. Do you realize that having that knowledge can get you terribly hurt, tortured or killed, and for more reasons than simply having crossed the SIE?"

"I—think so, sir." Dennis gulped to relieve the lump that had suddenly grown painfully large in his throat.

Karen clattered down the remaining steps and threw herself on the Penetrator's broad chest, arms encircling his neck. She began to cry. "Oh, I'm sorry. I didn't mean to say it. I truly didn't mean it. It—slipped out."

"It's Dennis you should apologize to, Karen. He's the one you endangered."

"Is it—really so serious?"

"I'm afraid so, son," the Penetrator informed Dennis.

The boy seemed brighten. "Then—since *they* know, I—I guess I'll have to live *here* to keep the secret?"

The Penetrator saw the fear driven from the orphan youngster's eyes and replaced by burgeoning hope. Suddenly, memories of Mark's own past clawed painfully at his heart. Thoughts of the long, unhappy months and years in the cold, loveless foster homes of his childhood exploded in Mark's brain and he had to swallow hard to ease the tension that clutched his larynx. "Are you that desperate to find a home, kid?"

It became Dennis's turn to break down. Large tears welled in his eyes and ran silently down his puffed-out cheeks. "Oh, yes, God yes. I so much want—to be—part of a family again—to—be someone." Without conscious direction he reached out to embrace Mark and Kevin, his loneliness giving strength to his arms.

"Uh—we'll have to—uh—see about that, ah, later." Mark found he had to keep clearing his throat. He took a deep breath and shook the mood from him. "First we have a small matter to clear up. Exactly what did you find in that office last night?"

Recovered from her remorse, Karen sat up and proudly displayed a sheaf of papers. "I brought it along with me. All about battle plans and stuff like that."

"Dennis says there's a safe too," Kevin added. "We got caught and then couldn't find anything else."

For the next half hour the Penetrator patiently drew from Dennis an account of life at the Carstairs Foundling Home. It presented a grim picture. From what Dennis recounted, the children had been subjected to some not-so-subtle brainwashing, well larded with Marxist doctrine and a hardcore leftist viewpoint of the world. The youngsters had been praised for proper responses and named as "liberators" in the coming world struggle. When he'd finished, Dennis added a final observation.

"It's funny. I knew what they were teaching us was a bunch of lies. I hated it. But the more I watched television, the more it seemed they weren't all that wrong. Like, people *are* starving and we *do* waste too much food and stuff here in this country. Then, when I got punished by being cut off TV, I got to hating them worse than before and I could see right through the bull that DiFalco put out. It was like—suddenly I saw things clear again."

"Subliminals," the Penetrator said aloud to himself.

"Huh?" the youngsters chorused.

"Hidden suggestions planted on television projections. Remember, the Aryan Brotherhood used the same method in Coalville?"

"Oh, yeah," Kevin responded. "Only it didn't work on some of us, 'cause we didn't drink the city water. They had to use drugs to make it effective."

"Do you think Meeks would have overlooked that at the orphanage?" the Penetrator inquired gently.

The realization struck the three children at once. "Drugs!" Dennis squeaked. "Ugh, what a bummer. Taking drugs is dumb."

"Gosh," Kevin gushed. "You poor kid. That is bad news. Say—" Kevin's excitement continued to rise. "Ain't this enough for now? I mean, we've been goin' at it for more'n a half hour. It's hot-tub time."

"A-l-l r-i-g-h-t!" Dennis seconded.

"*Isn't* this," Angie corrected her son from the archway to the dinette. "And I'll tell you something, young man. There may not be any more hot tub, or swimming pool, or skating rink for you for some time. I haven't yet decided how to punish you two for what you did last night."

"Aawh, Mo-o-m. It wasn't all that bad," Kevin protested.

"It wasn't? Why, you—nearly—got—your-selves—k-killed." Tears welled in Angie's eyes and she angrily blinked them away. "Oh, damn, there I go getting mother hennish again." She caught control of her emotions along with a deep breath and smiled at her offspring. "All right. You won this time. It's the hot tub, then *huevos rancheros*, bacon, and melon for breakfast."

"Far out!" Kevin enthused. The three children stampeded for the stairwell. Angie's voice halted them in a wild collision.

"Just this once, in deference to your guest, don't you think you might wear your swimsuits?"

"Why?" Dennis asked innocently. "I didn't bring one along."

"Kids!" Angie huffed in maternal helplessness. Then she turned on Mark. "Are you laughing at all this, mister?"

"N-no," the Penetrator managed through his attempt to stifle a guffaw. "As a matter of fact, I was struggling to keep from bawling like a baby." He quickly filled Angie in on the tautly emotional scene generated by the revelation of his identity as the Penetrator.

"Awh, the poor kid," Angie sympathized. "Can't we do something for him, honey? I mean right now? After what you told me about your own childhood, I can see how you must feel for him. Isn't there some way?"

"It's certain he'll have to live with someone who

is inside the secret. Someone who can constantly remind him of the danger involved if he ever let the slightest hint out. First things first, though. I've got to contact Dan Griggs and fill him in on what I have so far. Dennis will have to wait."

Something didn't seem right. The Penetrator thought. Don had been hot to get him involved in this affair, now he had turned cool and downright...

# 10

## THEY CALL IT RED TAPE

"So there you have it, Dan," the Penetrator told Dan Griggs over the telephone half an hour later. "Even the kids at the orphanage knew their guards were Korean. They used a variety of sterile arms, including Polish, French, and American, which indicates it's somebody's intelligence service. Add all that to the titles and contents of the two training schedules I saw and the conclusion is obvious."

"How's that?" Dan returned blandly. His attitude during Mark's report had been distant and somewhat reproving.

"C'mon, Dan. When Koreans are involved and the document is identified as 'Invasion Scenario for the DMZ,' and the direction of the invading force is south, it can't be anyone but the *North* Koreans. Somehow the SIE has tied up with the North Korean army, to play a little game of conquest. From the looks of it, they plan to use the children they are training as shock troops or, far more horrible, like the Cong used them in 'Nam."

"Aren't you jumping to some rather large conclusions, Arrowsmith?"

Something didn't scan right, the Penetrator thought. Dan had been hot to get him involved in this and now he had turned cool and downright obstructive. "What is it, Dan? Why all of a sudden do you seem to think I've been smoking wacky tobaccky or relating you some other kind of pipe dreams?"

"I didn't say that," Dan hedged. "You've done a fine job, so far, developed some valuable information. Only . . ."

"Something tells me I'm not going to like your 'only.' "

"It's—sort of, ah, involved, fella. My hands are tied. In fact, the government hasn't any alternatives open at this time. Anything you're working on now is only so much spinning of wheels. I'm sorry, but that's how it is."

Dangerous fires flared in the Penetrator's eyes. "What the hell is this? What alternatives are you talking about and why can't they be pursued?" An embarrassed silence followed Mark's outburst. "You owe me, Dan."

Griggs cleared his throat, spoke hesitantly. "I've got my orders direct from the attorney general. The Justice Department is no longer officially interested in the matter. And, no, it hasn't been taken over by the FBI, CIA, State, or Defense."

"How can that happen?" The Penetrator had a sinking feeling he knew only too well.

"It has, buddy. The *Société Internationale d'Élite,* in spite of recent changes in the government, still has a great number of friends on the Hill."

"Spell it out for me."

Dan's voice sounded uncomfortable. "I hope

this is a safe phone. If not, I'll be looking for work before noon. All right. The bottom line is this. All efforts at investigating this affair have been effectively blocked for the time being by certain ranking persons in Congress and entrenched Civil Service bureaucrats who are believed to owe favors to, or are members of, SIE."

"Shit!"

"Precisely. We're being drowned in that ever familiar sea of red tape. I'm as unhappy about it as you are." Dan slammed his fist on his desk, grunted with irritation. He decided to take a long chance. "Officially, *you can do nothing more* on this assignment—if you get my meaning."

"I, ah, think I do. Well, Dan, it was fun while it lasted. It's another reason, though, that I don't like doing favors for you. Things like this usually end up going bad."

"I don't know anything about that, either. Officially that is. I—I'm going to see the man at the other end of Pennsylvania Avenue from the Hill. I'll get back to you if anything changes."

"Then I guess that wraps it. Oh, yeah, one other little thing. I don't want to be prying, so snap my head off if I go overboard. Are you and Marge still thinking of adding on a family?"

"I—don't know, fella. We're getting a little old to take care of a baby."

"How about a part-grown one? Let me tell you about him. He's bright as Kell-light and his name is Dennis . . ."

"You're leaving," Angie accused an hour later in her bedroom while Mark packed his suitcase.

"Yes."

"May I inquire why?"

"The bureaucrats and the bunglers screwed it up again. As of now, no one is going after the SIE on this thing but me."

"Why does it have to be you?"

"Because, by God, I'm not going to see those kids slaughtered for the greater glory of North Korea and the SIE."

"Ah! The one-man-army bit again, eh?" Suddenly her eyes filled with tears and she threw herself into Mark's open arms. "Oh, I'm being bitchy and I hate it, but—but I don't want to see you hurt. I love you and I don't want to lose you. I—I . . ."

Mark gently stroked Angie's glossy, silken hair, feeling himself stirred by the sensual perfection of the shape of her head. "Hang in there, Angie. You and Kevin and Karen are very precious to me. I'm more worried about something happening to you. I'll be moving fast and hitting hard. The SIE won't have time to find me if I'm free to move on."

"Why can't you use our place as a base of operations?"

"There's no guarantee I won't leave tracks that can be followed to my lair. If I change location every time, no one can track me down. It's a simple matter of tactics—hit and run."

Angie recovered her former poise, fussed about rearranging her face. "Forgive my outburst?"

"Of course I do."

"I love you, Mark."

"And I love you, Angie, more than I should."

"Don't—please let's not have a maudlin farewell scene."

The Penetrator thought a moment about the

deep, abiding love this woman had for him and the anguish so plain in her eyes. "There's nothing you can do on the paperwork for Dennis until at least Monday, or when Dan gets here, so it looks like you have a houseguest."

"I don't mind, he's sweet."

"Then why don't you take the kids somewhere for the day and when you get back, I'll be—gone."

"They'll want to say good-bye."

"All right. I'll take a few minutes with each one of them before you leave."

The Penetrator made his first stop the Carstairs Foundling Home. The authorities had removed all the children and sealed the building as a crime scene. Their efforts made little interference for Mark. He entered the building, opened the hidden safe with aid of his electronic gadget that amplified tumbler noises, and obtained a wealth of information.

Not only did he find a list of other instructions involved in the scheme, but a notification from someone named Gore Sasson that the first shipment of children was to be made from the West Coast in less than a week. In fact, only four days remained. Mark also obtained confirmation that the youngsters were to be used as assassins and terrorist units, with the oldest and best trained incorporated into the invasion as shock troops. How to stop it?

Part of Mark's mind argued that the way to strike the most effective blow would be to cut off the head of the dragon. Killing David Felder, logic contradicted, would only present a temporary delay. Felder was merely the surface head of SIE.

Behind him must exist a governing board of some sort. A new front man would be selected, along with a huge public spectacle funeral to make Felder a martyr, and it would be business as usual. Somehow he had to create so much notice of this particularly outrageous scheme that all the influence of all the SIE members in the world could no longer maintain a cover-up.

Hit the training schools of these kiddie killers.

The answer came in a clear burst of reason without conscious effort. Sure. He could do it. Involve the local law, police departments, sheriff's offices, state investigators, and, most of all, the local press. That should create enough yowling and howling and a few corpses of SIE agents to throw the entire time table off schedule. By then, the Feds would have to move in. The Penetrator checked his list of orphanages.

He'd head first to Moab and the Queen of Angels Missionary School.

Omar Koyne didn't see what he was doing as a criminal act. He didn't have an evil bone in his body. The thought that—so long as he allowed certain subjects and instructors into his private orphanage—the money would keep on flowing from the Felder Foundation further soothed his conscience. Why, he'd been on the verge of bankruptcy when a friend and colleague, Arnold Meeks in Salt Lake City, had suggested he write a grant request and submit it to the foundation.

To his surprise, it had been accepted. Along with the endless funds that now flowed into his Miles City Youth Refuge, came conditions. The content of courses taught the children altered considerably. Koyne hadn't objected, the new slant agreed quite nicely with his own views. Then came the paramilitary training and he had protested. He was vehemently opposed to violence and the brutish, dehumanizing nature of military service of any sort. Why, hadn't he even been an activist in the fight against atomic weapons and nuclear power? Omar Koyne then found out that the new faculty members sent to him were aware of certain embarrassing aspects of his private life.

Like Arnold Meeks, Omar maintained a far more intimate interest in the children under his control than the normal, healthy outlook of an orphanage director should encompass. He would, Omar painfully recalled being told, keep his mouth shut regarding any and all changes instituted by the newcomers and in return he would be allowed to indulge himself in pursuit of his pederastic pleasures. The memory caused Omar to once again sigh heavily in resignation.

Seated comfortably in his apartment at the Miles City orphanage, Omar reached into the drawer of an end table and took out a large photo album. He opened the cover and looked avidly at the naked loveliness of his favorites. Ah, yes, such beauty. Larry and Nancy, Joey and Jamie and little Patti. Omar's head jerked up at a faint sound that seemed to come from his kitchen. He listened intently a second.

Nothing.

Omar went back to a perusal of his garden of homegrown delights, as he called his small victims. He turned two more pages, then froze when his senses janglingly told him that another person had entered the room. Omar looked up this time into the muzzle end of a MAC silencer.

The fat, bulky tube only two feet from his face seemed to have a hole nearly half an inch in diameter at its end. With a start, Omar realized he was looking at some sort of weapon. The grim, hawk-nosed face and powerful body of the man behind it left him no doubt that real trouble had come at last. Omar's insides turned to icy slush and beads of oily fear sweat popped out on his bald pate.

"I—I've never said anything about your operation here," Omar protested in a strangled bleat. "Honestly. And I don't c-care what you do here."

"I'm not one of those scumbags, Omar," the Penetrator told him quietly. "I want the names and whereabouts of every one of the instructors involved in the SIE program here."

Quickly Omar told him.

"Now, what about guards?"

"T-there are five of them on duty at all times. Ugly Korean brutes who don't even speak English."

"I've already accounted for the two outside. Where will I find the other three?"

Omar lost no time in providing the information.

"Thank you, Omar. Good-bye."

The Sidewinder submachine gun spoke three times, quieted to a gentle chuffing by the big silencer. The slugs entered Omar's face and throat and exploded bits of him over the high back of his wing chair. The Penetrator picked up Omar's photo album, put it in a big manila envelope, ad-

dressed it to the county sheriff, and tucked it under his arm. Then he went hunting for the remaining serpents in this nest of vipers.

Baylor Boy's Ranch had operated for thirty
years. Old Roy Baylor, who had founded it, had
long since sold out to other interests, who had en-
larged the facility and taken in more students. Not
an orphanage, the school catered to "trou-
bled boys" whose parents could afford private
care rather than a state-sponsored reformatory. It
offered psychological counseling in addition to
grades three through twelve, horseback riding,
swimming, and tennis. Tommy Cross had come to
Baylor at the age of nine. Now, eight years later,
he remained at his own request, his tuition paid by
a "scholarship" fund from the Felder Foundation.

Tommy had duty as sergeant of the guard the
night the Penetrator hit Baylor. Mark had struck at
orphanages in Moab and Miles City and that day
used his state ID to make a soft recon of the boy's
ranch. He identified the SIE instructors and, when
he came back, easily located them and elimi-
nated all three. Then he slipped among the buildings of the ranch proper until he reached a large
hay barn.

A few matches and a can of gasoline provided
all the Penetrator needed to set a blaze that
would be sure to attract fire and police units.
Tommy Cross smelled smoke almost immediately
and, in accordance with his orders, went to investigate. He spotted the Penetrator when Mark
made a short dash through an open space in
front of a corral.

"Halt!" Tommy commanded. He swung up his

short, U.S. M-1 carbine and fired a shot that screamed off a steel hinge into the night. Immediately the remainder of the guard force rushed toward the scene of the disturbance.

"Fire in the hay barn. Call the fire department," Tommy told them. "Bobby, Tim, you come with me." Tommy started out at a trot after the intruder, whom he'd only glanced for a moment. Ahead of him, the Penetrator rounded the corner of a building and jogged into the darkness, across a field that would take him to the fence that bordered the road.

"Stop right there, mister, or I'll shoot you."

The Penetrator found himself confronted by three youngsters about twelve years old. Each of them competently held a weapon. The middle one pointed his unwaveringly at Mark's belly.

"Take it easy with those guns, kids. I don't want to hurt any of you because you don't know what it is you're mixed up in."

"Goddamned imperialist spy!" the boy in the center yelled, eyes blank and face contorted in fury. "Capitalist tool, warmonger, your days are numbered."

The kid was going to kill him, Mark realized. The tiny, nail-bitten finger tightened to whiteness on the trigger of the diminutive Czech Model 61, 7.65mm submachine gun. Mark forced down his revulsion and reluctance at harming a mere child and fired a three-round burst from the Sidewinder.

The trio of big .45 slugs tore into the short, skinny little boy's legs. He screamed and fell. His two companions, filled with horror of their first-hand introduction to violence, dropped their firearms and ran into the darkness. Quickly the Penetrator climbed over the fence and hurried toward his car.

"I thought you'd be headed here," Tommy Cross's voice grated out of the blackness beside the road. The Penetrator had only a split second to dive forward and roll on the ground before the yellow-orange muzzle flesh of Tommy's carbine briefly illuminated the area and a .30-caliber bullet screeched off the bumper of the rental Aspen.

The Penetrator came up facing back toward his assailant. He cut loose with three closely spaced bursts from the Sidewinder. Tommy Cross screamed in agony when the low-flying slugs bit into the tender flesh of his abdomen and destroyed one kidney, his bladder, and the renal artery. He sent another round from the carbine skyward and then pitched face-first into the stygian night of eternity.

Quickly Mark climbed behind the wheel of the Aspen and sped off into the darkness. The boy's ranch had been in a higher state of readiness than the previous institutions he'd visited. There hadn't been any Korean guards around. Some of the more advanced juvenile assassins apparently handled those duties. And, oh, God, he'd killed one kid. Sick from the enormous burden this hopeless mission had placed upon him, the Penetrator drove on toward Provo and another raid on an SIE school for kiddie killers.

# 11

## CROSS-COUNTRY KILL

"He's getting too close *now,* damnit," David Felder railed into the mouthpiece of the ivory, French-style telephone in his New York office.

"I'll put more men on it," Colonel Gee responded.

"No. Don't do that. Your operatives will have too high a profile in a Western country. They'd stand out to him like a lump of coal on snow. Six of our installations he's hit—six! The schedule can't be compromised."

"These things take time."

"That's something we don't have, colonel. Your government's setting the pace. I want you to put some kids on it. You've got enough of them trained now. Turn the little monsters loose on that son of a bitch. We know where he's headed. Get them out on every highway in the area. Find him and kill him." Before Colonel Gee could make a response, Felder slammed the handset back on its gold cradle.

The Penetrator rolled along I-80N, a few miles over the border into Idaho. He felt tried and utterly drained of any ability to continue to face the smiling-faced, innocent-looking assassins. He'd attacked six of the SIE's terrorist schools in three nights and had been forced to kill three older teenagers. He did have a direction, though, to go with the ominous notation that the first of the programmed juvenile killers would leave the next day. Seattle.

The SIE had established a safe house to store their orphan army at an old movie theater near Pioneer Square. If he drove all day, and through into the next, he'd barely have time to make it. He checked the Fuzz Buster radar detector he'd installed the day before and nudged the car up to eighty.

Speed, motion, and silence became hypnotic. The Penetrator stopped in Jerome for coffee and a steak sandwich. A few miles out of town the wide interstate reverted to a narrow, two lane, state-maintained highway. Three miles down the road, Mark came across a small boy trying to hitch a ride. His conscience, burdened by the memory of the youngster he'd had to kill in his battle with the SIE, gave a twinge. He slowed and pulled onto the dusty verge and waited for the kid to catch up.

"You goin' all the way into Bliss, Mister?" the lad asked, rubbing one bare foot over the other.

"Sure am."

"Good. I'm going in to the Boys' Club for a swim." He gestured with a towel he clutched tightly in one hand. He looked to be about ten or eleven, lots of freckles and carroty hair. He had an engaging smile that reminded Mark of Dennis Roberts.

"Hop in." Mark waited for an eighteen-wheeler to thunder past, rocking the small Aspen, then pulled out into the lane. The kid kept fumbling with his towel. Mark decided to put him at ease.

"My name's Greg, what's yours?"

"Ronny. Ronny Horton."

"You live on a farm around here, Ronny?"

"Nuh—yeah. Yeah, I do."

A mile down the road, Ronny suddenly pulled a wicked looking push dagger from inside the roll of towel and lunged across the seat at the Penetrator.

A searing pain flashed across Mark's chest when the sharp blade slid through cloth and cut a fiery line into the skin covering his ribs. Ronny had the same mild, sweetly innocent look on his face Mark had seen on all of the other SIE-conditioned robots. In automatic reaction to the attack, the Penetrator lashed out with his fist and caught Ronny in the temple. At the same instant he slammed on the brake.

Ronny's head smashed into the dashboard. He fell to the floorboards unconscious. Mark swerved to the side of the road, opened the door, and tossed the kid to the gravel.

At least he didn't have to kill that one. He sped on, anxious to get to Boise, where he'd been told he could pick up a commuter flight to Seattle.

At Sea-Tac, the large, international airport that serviced the Seattle-Tacoma area, the Penetrator retrieved his luggage, rented a car, and entered the city on I-5. Memory served him well and he located a parking garage off Pioneer Square. Two minutes later he stood on the sidewalk, across the street from the Puget Theatre.

ALL "G" PROGRAM—OPEN 10 AM; large red letters spelled the message on the marquee. That would provide excellent cover for a lot of children coming and going, the Penetrator thought. While he observed, a group of youngsters clustered near the box office. The Penetrator crossed the street, bought a ticket, and entered the theater.

Mark knew that mixed among the trained kiddie killers would be a large number of innocent children and not a few adults. The SIE team operating this safe house could not feed and provide sleeping space for their charges in a movie house. There had to be some connection between this building and another. He decided to search for it first on the mezzanine level, where the rest rooms and manager's officer were located.

Outside the men's room, three short, stocky Koreans jumped the Penetrator.

To Mark's left, the closest man dropped low into the crouching leg attack position of *kwonpup*. One fist lashed out to strike a nerve center while the other feinted to snare the Penetrator's right leg.

The Penetrator saw through the ruse and kicked the man in the face. His head snapped back and he rolled with the blow, staggered but not knocked out. The other two Koreans launched a simultaneous attack.

Mark countered the guard on his right with a *yoko hijiate* side elbow strike, then executed a forward roll to escape his second opponent. The *tae kwan do* trained Orientals surged.

Ui Mi, a tough little lieutenant in the North Korean security service, was a student of the *Songkae* school. He began a series of distinctly Chinese-origin circular hand movements similar to the style of the late Bruce Lee. He warbled, twittered, and whistled, making animal sounds, until the Penetrator hit him in the throat with a dragon fist, *furi zuki* flare punch.

The Korean spook stumbled backward, one hand clutching his ruined Adam's apple while blood from his savaged voice box bubbled from his mouth. Unable to breathe, he soon lost consciousness and slid down the wall to assume a sitting position, head resting among the cigarette butts in the white sand of a stand-type ashtray. The Penetrator had no time to watch Ui Mi's departure from this world.

A spray of wet, red drops told him that the man he'd kicked in the face had returned to the fight.

Blood streaming from his ruined nose, Injong Choi came at the Penetrator with flailing fists and feet. He might have succeeded in his attack if the remaining gook hadn't decided to launch his own offensive at the same time. The Penetrator ducked low, pivoted to one side, and the two Koreans slammed into each other. The Penetrator decided the odds now indicated a quick ending.

The Penetrator rose abruptly and threw his right leg backward. Before the struggling men could disentangle themselves, Mark released a *mawashi geri* roundhouse kick.

The blow came in low and caught Sergeant Hauhn under the armpit. He stumbled backward, arms windmilling to regain balance. He struck the railing around the stairwell and toppled over. Superb training kept him quiet during his fall and an eerie silence came from the open space until Hauhn struck the bannister below.

The cracking of his spine sounded loud in the stillness.

"Yi-i-i-i-i-i!" Injong Choi charged the Penetrator, who solved this final threat by the simple expedient of drawing his Star PD and shooting Choi twice in the chest.

"Fire!" someone shouted from below. Frightened voices took up the call and then screams of terror rose from the crowded theater when billows of smoke began to crowd out into the lobby. Someone had deliberately set off a blaze.

Panic swelled through the busy movie house. People ran from place to place, seeking escape. Coughing children poured from the balcony, swarming around the Penetrator like the flotsam on an incoming tide. Screams rose from below. Fire-alarm bells rang shrilly from the area of the refreshment stand. Amidst all the confusion the Penetrator suddenly discovered the secret of how to get into the SIE safe house.

Starting as individuals, tightly disciplined children, unaffected by the pandemonium around them, began to gravitate toward the men's room. They formed into loose ranks and went inside, boys and girls alike. The Penetrator followed.

At the far end of the room Mark saw a section of wall swinging closed behind the last pair in line. Quickly he dashed to the pivoting door and forced it open. On the other side he saw the biggest man he had ever encountered.

Barefoot, dressed only in the greenish-brown uniform trousers and billed forage cap of the North Korean army, the huge solider towered six foot seven and must have weighed nearly four hundred pounds. The smooth, effortless way he swung his rifle toward the Penetrator indicated he had little surplus fat on his gigantic frame. He stamped his leading foot and bellowed in approved style for bayonet combat.

His first thrust missed and the Penetrator stepped inside the threat of cold steel. He pressed the muzzle of his Star PD against the hard flesh below the Korean's chin and squeezed the trigger.

A 185-grain JHP slug ripped through the man's tongue, crashed through the roof of his mouth, and blew off the top of his skull, lifting with it the forage cap and its red star decoration. For a moment the soldier stood in place, his eyes bulged from the hydrostatic shock, blood streaming from his half-open mouth. Then, in slow motion, he toppled forward.

In the narrow corridor, the Penetrator barely managed to evade the falling body. He started in pursuit of the juvenile assassins.

Fifty feet down the hall, Mark encountered a locked door. He shot his way in and, across the room, found another. He came to a third barrier and decided to use a little caution. From an angle that kept him away from the doorway, Mark fired three rounds into the lock mechanism of this obstruction. He hugged the wall while a fiery stream of bullets smashed through the center panel, sending showers of wood splinters into the room the Penetrator occupied. He made a quick mental calculation of expended ammunition.

Eight rounds. Five more and he would be on his third and final magazine, he reminded himself. Then he kicked the door open and dived through at a low angle.

Two short bursts from an automatic weapon chipped plaster and chewed gouges of wood from the doorframe. The Penetrator rolled to one side and located the machine gunner. He brought the Star PD to bear while more slugs tore into the floorboards around him and one bullet slapped painfully into the heel of his left shoe. Mark gently ticked off a round.

A squat, ugly Korean with a misshapen head and buck teeth dropped the MAT 49 French SMG he'd been using, threw both arms wide and pitched over the edge of a desk, sprawled across the green blotter, and began to stain it red. Another target quickly presented itself.

Red faced with fury, one of the robotized assassins, a boy of sixteen, leaped from behind a rank of filing cabinets. A Makarov 9mm auto-loader blazed in his left hand. One copper-jacketed ball round cracked over the Penetrator's head, close enough to clip a few stray hairs. Mark instinctively jerked downward and swung his .45 onto line.

A bellow of sound accompanied the fat muzzle bloom of the Star PD. Mark's bullet took the kid in the right hip, wrenching his leg bone from the socket.

"Unnngh!" the youth grunted. He dropped the Makarov and turned toward his injured side. Then his moan of pain turned to a howl of agony when his full weight came on the useless appendage.

"We give up! Don't shoot, don't shoot!" came a

wail of terror from a trio of the SIE kiddie killers huddled at one end of a long sofa.

"Hands in the air, then stand slowly," the Penetrator commanded. Cautiously they complied. "Who's in charge here?"

"He was." A fat, pimply-faced youngster with mousey brown hair pointed to the dead machine gunner.

"Who's your squad leader?"

"Him," the chubby would-be terrorist indicated the wounded sixteen-year-old who had lapsed into unconsciousness from shock.

"Where are the others?"

No longer under fire, the pudgy orphan-assassin began to regain some of his former zeal for the Cause. "It's too late, fucker. They're all gone—all but us."

"Where did they go? What are they using for transportation?"

No answer came. The boy's acne-ravaged face grew stubborn and his lips protruded wetly in an insolent pout. He crossed fat-jiggling arms over his blubbery chest and turned flat, blue eyes on the Penetrator in a hate-filled glare, then grunted his reply. "Get stuffed."

The Penetrator took careful aim and shot the kid through the thick roll of fat on his right side.

A soprano shriek of pain and terror ripped from the youngster's throat. He wet his pants and, his legs turned to spaghetti, he collapsed to the floor, sobbing in agony. The boy clasped both hands over the throbbing wound. Little blood flowed. The bullet had not entered his abdomen, merely smashed its way through layers of adipose tissue.

In rapid gulps the kid recovered enough to let the words spill out.

"I-in a-a air-p-plane. Th-th-three plane loads T-to-to N-north Korea."

"Everyone who was here?"

"Y-yeah. All but u-us."

"How many?"

"M-maybe two-three hundred all together. Them an' the guys in charge."

Up to three hundred programed assassins on the loose along the DMZ between North and South Korea. The idea boggled the Penetrator. He had to get out of this rapidly closing trap and find some way of stopping an unbelievable tragedy.

Fire and police sirens wailed outside. Time had dribbled away.

# 12

## JOURNEY ABROAD

"Dan, we've got a problem, the Penetrator told Dan Griggs over the phone twenty minutes later, after he managed to evade attention from the swarm of emergency vehicles and police outside the Puget Theatre.

"Where do you get this *'we'* stuff, Tonto?"

"All right, officially you're off the case. But unofficially I need some help." Quickly Mark explained the situation, including the destination of the children, brainwashed and motivated to kill American and South Korean soldiers. A long, two-second silence followed.

"Wheew! The shit's really hit the air-circulating machine. I'll do what I can from this end. They've got to stop for fuel somewhere, don't they? Maybe we can get them on the ground."

"Fat chance. If they follow the Arctic Circle route, which is the smartest thing considering their destination, they can put down anywhere in Canada and, with Communist diplomatic papers, be given the royal welcome."

"Maybe I can get Sec Def to scramble interceptors out of Alaska. The fly-boys can shoot them out of the sky."

"Jesus, Dan, these are kids! We want to stop them, break up the play, sure, but wholesale slaughter?"

"Okay, okay. I'm workin' on it, fella. Give a little."

"What I want is a clear way to get over there and finish it. Cut off the heads and the bodies will fall apart. All I need to do is eliminate Treavor DiFalco, a North Korean intelligence type named Gee, and Gore Sasson of the SIE. Then I can play pied piper and lead the kiddies over the line and into custody."

"You don't expect much, do you, buddy?"

"I've got one other source. If he goes for it, coordinate with him. I've got to leave Seattle today."

"Gotcha. And, ah," a catch came in Dan's voice, then it returned warm, rich, and vibrant. "I can never thank you enough, buddy, for Dennis. I brought him home yesterday. Marge and I love him madly."

The Penetrator hung up, his spirits suddenly lifted, a wide grin spread his face. He fished for more change and a telephone number from his wallet. Mark dialed, inserted the proper amount, and fought his way through one receptionist and two secretaries. At last his man came on the line.

"Well, goddamn! Don't tell me I've got that arrowhead flippin' supertrooper on the line?"

"Toro , is this line secure?" Toro Baldwin, in his Dallas office of the huge electronics firm for which he worked, chuckled heartily. "Hell, every line into this place is secure. What's on your mind?"

"You owe me one, Toro."

"You bet your sweet ass I do—after the way you

ducked out and let the other guys take all the credit for that Persis deal. The rescued hostages wanted to thank you too. So, shoot, sergeant. What can Concept Electronics do for you?"

"I'd prefer it was done by you, personally and most privately. I need to get into North Korea."

"Like I need a hole in the head."

"I'm serious. I have to be able to get in with enough ordnance to off three prime targets."

"You gonna fill me in?"

"After it's over."

"How much company do you want?"

"Little as possible. It's hairy and it's unofficial."

"What ain't, these days? I need more than you've given me to lay out the operation. Like, who's that important among those pip-squeak North Korean slope bastards?"

The Penetrator sensed that Baldwin, a former Colonel well accustomed to giving the orders, was fishing for more of the plan up front. Mark couched his answer carefully. "This isn't a Company job, Toro. What do you think of the SIE?"

"Those traitorous sons of bitches? I'd like to line 'em up against a wall, every parasite one of them, and blow their asses all the way from here to the hottest hubs of hell. Anyone who don't realize those bastards got their fat asses richer off 'Nam while we got ourselves killed—and then sold us out in the end to demoralize the survivors—has been goin' around with his head up his butt for the past ten years. And what makes me sick is they did it in the name of some cockamamy One World government scheme they're tryin' to foist off on the so-called intellectuals and the rest of the dimwits." Toro abruptly stopped and gulped a deep breath. "Awh, crap. There I go makin' like a soapbox radical."

The Penetrator had heard the fiery retired colonel's opinions before. Major Leizenka of the KGB had caled Baldwin a reactionary, right-wing, redneck bull. But then, the Penetrator dismissed it, Communists were used to thinking in such terms. "Then that means your people will set it up for me?"

"Hell, yes. Grab a flight to Tokyo. Get back to me with your flight number and I'll have one of my men there to meet you."

"Thanks, Toro. Now, coordinate this through Dan Griggs." He gave Baldwin the number. "Dan will be at that phone until the operation is over. I really appreciate all this, Toro."

"Hell, boy, it's the least I could do for you."

At the end of a routine JAL flight to Japan —shrimp and vegatable tempura, rice, *sake* and strawberries dipped in powdered sugar, accompanied by samisen and koto music—the Penetrator was met by Toro Baldwin's man in Ja pan, Tommy Yamato. With Tommy was an unusu ally tall, slender, athletic-looking young Oriental whom he introduced to Mark as Kim Suŏng Ree.

"He's going in with you. Toro's idea," Tommy explained.

"Why?" the Penetrator demanded.

"You don't speak Korean, do you?" Kim observed.

"No."

"Then the subject's closed," Tommy concluded.

The Penetrator gave Kim a closer look, evaluating him as a fighting man. He liked what he saw.

Kim appeared relaxed, yet his eyes roved constantly over persons passing close by and his body had the economy of motion of an experienced soldier. They could, the Penetrator decided, work together. The iron-hardness exhibited a moment before by Tommy Yamato caused Mark to rate him as a takeover kind of guy. There seemed something familiar about Tommy that tugged at Mark's memory.

Then he had it. Tommy, a short, slightly built third-generation Japanese-American, reminded Mark of Uchi Takayama, with whom he'd served in the army and shared several adventures since. Nowhere near as voluble as Uchi, Tommy Yamato got right to the point.

Tommy helped Mark retrieve his single piece of luggage and escorted him to a waiting car. All the while the young contact man cast nervous glances around as though expecting to be arrested at any moment. Once in the vehicle, speeding away from Haneda Airport, the Penetrator commented on it.

"What's the matter, Tommy?"

"You. That's the matter. At least you had better sense than to try to bring any weapons into the country. Even so, the stuff the Old Man told us to gather for you could put us all away in a Jap prison for the rest of our lives."

"Sorry about that."

"Look, you're just a visiting fireman, so to speak. But the rest of us have to live with things the way they are. Japan has some of the strictest and stupidest gun laws in the world. Only a select few can own a rifle or shotgun and no one, but no none, can own a handgun, except the government. Yet, the *Yakuza*—Japan's criminal brotherhood, like the Mafia—have any kind of firearm you might want. Hell, *we* bought the submachine gun and silencers you wanted from them."

"Don't the authorities prosecute the *Yakuza* for firearms violations when they catch them?"

"Not so's you'd notice. Only people like us."

"Relax, Tommy," Kim interjected. "It's the same wherever that kind of fuzzy-minded thinking prevails."

Tommy Yamato ran a hesitant hand across his brow and studied Mark Hardin in the garish, flickering neon light of the Ginza. "I don't know who you really are, Greg Miller, or what you're up to, but I'll be glad when we deliver you and your guns to North Korea and get shut of you."

Half an hour later, at an airport on the northwest side of Tokyo, the Penetrator, Tommy, and Kim climbed aboard a rickety DC-3 already loaded with the supplies Mark had specified. The airframe must have over a hundred thousand hours on it, Mark surmised with a shudder and wondered about the condition of the engines. The twin fans coughed to life with a healthy enough roar and the ancient cargo plane rolled down the runway.

Once airborne, the Penetrator shouted to be heard above the rattling, creaking sounds of the tired bird and the bellow of its engines. "How about filling me in on what's laid on?"

"Oh," Tommy Yamato returned lightly, now that they were airborne and out of the jurisdiction of the Tokyo police. "We have to go to Hakodate first. The junk you are going to use is part of a fleet maintained by Concept Electronics to install and maintain new undersea cables of optical fibers for telephone communication between Hokkaido and Honshu islands. No way we could have brought it down here to make the narrow crossing between Matsue and Kyongju. You could have made it in by way of South Korea then. Of course, that would have taken a couple of more days."

"Which I don't have."

"Just so. You'll pass through the Tsugaru Strait and cross the Inland Sea, taking advantage of prevailing currents and winds and hopefully make landfall a few miles north of Kosong. From there it's up to you."

"Kosŏng's right close on the thirty-eighth parallel, isn't it?"

"Toro said we were going to operate near the DMZ. Tommy planned it to put us close to the action," Kim informed Mark.

"How long will the crossing take?"

"With luck, a day and a half. That's a net saving of three days over the other route," Tommy took up the briefing.

"I'm grateful for that."

Increasing turbulence drew the Penetrator's attention. He peered through a small window behind his sling-strap seat and noticed a wide expanse of the horizon obscured by gathering masses of dense clouds. Among them he saw a profusion of towering, swirling thunderheads. Someone was in for a huge storm. He fervently hoped it would speed across the islands and not along the course he and Kim would follow. Two and a half hours later, the DC-3 let down at Hakodate. They reached the harbor without incident.

The Penetrator supervised the stowing of his

gear aboard the junk. The *Kaki Kara Maru* the Penetrator thought to be an appropriate sobriquet when Tommy explained the vessel's name in English. An oyster shell on a storm-tossed sea. It fit. When the crew at last cast off bow and stern lines, a rain squall swept over the harbor. The Penetrator shivered and joined Kim below to change into more suitable clothing. It promised to be a grand voyage.

"*Takai o tachimas'*," Tommy Yamato saluted from the rainshrouded pier to the men going below. "Stand tall."

The Penetrator appreciated the gesture. They'd need all the well-wishes they could get.

An hour out beyond the Tsugaru Strait, the junk encountered a following sea. With each horizon-obscuring swell, the sterncastle rose, wallowed like a duck settling onto water, then descended with a stomach-wrenching crunch. The wind, quartering toward the stern now, increased steadily in velocity. Low, scudding clouds thickened, grew angry black green. The radio operator came onto deck and hurried to where his captain and the Penetrator stood near the wheel.

"Tokyo weather radio predicts gale-force winds, captain."

"What strength?"

Hopelessly the sailor cast a worried glance aft, to the dark line of storm that rapidly approached. "Force Four—or Five, captain."

Kim translated the bad news for the Penetrator. Then he added, his face waxy green. "And oh, God, do I get seasick."

Mark, too, studied the worsening conditions. "We can't turn back and we can't head to the nearest port. Go on—that's the only choice."

The captain shouted his orders in Japanese, "All hands to shorten sail." Barefooted seamen rushed onto deck and turned to their tasks. Time sped all too quickly by until the first fat spatters of rain fell on the junk. The wind, lashing with the cutting edge of a knife, howled in the rigging. The sailors bent to their lines.

One thick manila cord parted with an explosive pop and suddenly Mark's vision grew restricted to a matter of two feet. Green spume, foam flecked, crashed aboard over the stern rail and the junk began violently to pitch and roll. Furious gusts of wind and sheets of rain pummeled everyone on deck. Too late, the captain yelled his next order.

"Drop the mainsail!"

Wedged by uneven wind pressure, the boom swung at the top first, a fraction of a second after the hands let go the lines. The lower crosspiece followed erratically a moment later. Bellied by the raging gale, the sail strained to capacity, exceeded all bonds, and let go with a thunderous rumble and stuttering flutter. The stays and booms recoiled in opposite directions, throwing three seamen, shrieking, into the madly driving waves.

"*Tetsudaimas' ka!*" others of the struggling crew cried for help.

"*Minna wa ushinaimas' deska!*" the helmsman screamed as the following pressure of the madly lashing waves tore the spokes of the wheel from his hands. "All is lost!"

The captain jerked away from the precarious

protection of a running line and flung himself at the wildly spinning control and the frightened man who stood paralyzed behind it. He slapped the helmsman with resounding force.

"Let her swing!" he yelled over the violence of the storm. "Bring her around and head into the blow."

Overhead, transmitted from the very roots of the stout mast, the vibrations and erratic gyrations of the ship translated into a corkscrew effect that wrenched stout wood fibers one from the embrace of another. Unable to maintan integrity in the face of such unfettered nature, the mast parted halfway up.

A sailor screamed and died, impaled by one long splinter of the severed, mobile portion of the mast. It plunged toward the deck with ponderous grace and smashed partway through before it toppled unevenly toward the starborad rail, which it crushed to slivers before trailing all its useless rigging and shards of sail into the tossing sea.

A pallor of sickly green drained the captain of all expression. He swung himself from stanchion to stanchion until he reached the area of greatest damage. The Penetrator and Kim came along behind. A quick look was all the experienced sailing master needed. He turned to face his unwonted passengers.

His words, hesitant at first, ended in a resigned rush. "*Honto ni—minna wa ushinaimas' desks, nēi*" He recovered himself enough to repeat in English for Mark's sake, "Truly, all is lost, you see?"

The Penetrator shouted into the icy teeth of the

tumultuous storm to be heard, while the tiny, vulnerable wooden junk pitched and heeled in a frenzy. His words, blown to shreds by the storm, could not help but agree.

# 13

## HOSTILE SHORES

With the bow pointed directly into the lashing gale, the helmsman managed to regain control of the rudder. Down below, two crewmen struggled to get the auxiliary engine running.

A thick plume of black diesel smoke belched from the stack, to be dashed into thin shards by the near typhoon. The engine snorted and settled into the baritone, heartbeatlike *lub-dub* of a marine power plant. A crucial minute dragged by, then a second, and the helmsman called to the captain.

"We have steerage way, captain."

"Hold her steady. We have to clear this debris."

An hour's hard work, made more difficult by the churning sea, went by before the broken mast had been cut free of its trailing obstructions and lashed securely to the deck. A thoroughly seasick Kim appeared briefly in the hatchway, groaned with eloquent example of his misery, and went back below. More time passed and, with it, an imperceptible change began.

Without slackening, the wind began to shift,

point by point, until it blew back in the direction from which it had originally come. By gradual increments, the junk began to drift northwestward, toward the hostile shore of the Kamchatka near the port of Vladivostok. When the peak fury of the storm abated slightly, the captain managed a rough estimate of their heading and course and turned to the Penetrator with a look of despair.

"There is nothing we can do about it until the weather moderates. We are being pushed into Soviet waters."

"What if you keep the bow into the storm?"

"The effect of wind and tide will move us even though we have speed enough to control the rudder. To quarter the storm is to invite being capsized."

"I don't want to sound inane, Captain Heida," the Penetrator told him, "but if we can't turn back and we can't go on, all we can do is hang in there and hope for the best."

A deep sigh escaped the short, tough Japanese. "You Americans are like Confucius. You have a saying for everything."

An hour before dawn, the tempest blew itself out. Everyone aboard, except the relief helmsman, took a hurried nap to recover part of their strength. A lot of work lay ahead of them.

Sudden, pervading silence woke the Penetrator half an hour later. He immediately realized that what had jolted him out of the utter depths of fatigued slumber had been the stuttering of the engine when it gave its last lurching cycle before giving out, the sound of which seemed to echo in the corridors of his mind. He swung his feet off the bunk and came face to face with Kim. The young Korean's face crumpled with worry.

"If I'm taken by the Soviets, I'll be shot outright. You they might save to trade for one of their own."

"We're not going to be captured," the Penetrator stated with more assurance than he felt. "Let's go on deck."

With the exception of the two men assigned to maintain and operate the junk's power plant, the remainder of the crew worked to reshape the broken piece of mast and outfit it for restepping. The Penetrator and Kim joined in the labor. Within twenty minutes the self-appointed cook came on deck with heavy mugs of hot tea. He followed it with bowls of rice balls and a thick, pungent fish sauce. The crew ate and returned to its labors.

"Mast on the starboard horizon," came the lookout's call an hour later.

"Can you make her out?" Captain Heida asked anxiously. He'd been able to complete a sunrise sighting with his sextant, using the sun and position of Venus to verify their position. Only the Penetrator had been taken into his confidence. The bobbing, now helpless junk lay six miles off the shore of the Kamchatka Penninsula, well inside Russian waters, some eleven miles north of the entrance of Vladivostok harbor.

"Looks like a fishing trawler, sir."

"Not so good. Half the time they're patrol boats disguised as fishermen," the captain observed to Mark, who stood at the rail nearby, fastening a thick running block to a belaying line.

"Should I break out the weapons?"

The captain blanched. "Good God, no. If it is a

patrol craft, they could blow us out of the water before we got off a shot."

Slowly the Russian craft bore down on the wallowing junk. With each minute, details came clearer. After fifteen minutes, the captain breathed a sigh of relief. "She looks genuine enough, but we won't know until she gets here."

Seventeen anxiety-filled minutes later, while the crew worked frantically to complete repairs, the trawler hove to alongside. The captain, in a heavy sea coat and karakul hat, raised an electric bullhorn to his lips.

"*Kateet'ye pamohshnee?*"

"No, thank you," the junk's captain returned in passable Russian. "We are effecting our own repairs."

"*Kakoy vee nats'yonalnostee?'* " the Russian captain demanded, although he could clearly see the name of the ship and the Japanese flag flying.

"We are Japanese," came the dutiful reply.

"Throw us a line and we will tow you to Vladivostok."

"No need for that," Captain Heida responded. "We should be under motor power any minute now." To emphasize his words, a thick cloud of smoke erupted from the stack and the engine limped reluctantly to life.

"Are you sure you will be all right? You are in Soviet waters and it is our duty to escort you in—though I am more inclined to get on with my fishing. I hailed you as a courtesy of the sea. Will you check in with the authorities on your own before departing Soviet waters?"

"*Da, da!*" Captain Heida yelled over the widening distance between vessels as the junk got under way. "*N'yet b'yespakoyt'yes! Oooydeet'yeh*—Go away," he added under his breath.

The Soviet fisherman waved cheerfully and the engine room telegraph bell could be heard ringing over the gently lapping waves.

It might be well and good to tell the trawler captain not to worry about it, the Penetrator thought as he gusted out a breath he'd apprehensively held for the past minute. For his own part, he felt he'd worried enough for both of them. He stepped over to Captain Heida.

"That was close." At the captain's grim nod, Mark went on. "Next stop North Korea, eh, captain?"

"Right you are, Mr. Miller."

Although the *Kaki Kara Maru* sailed southward, Captain Heida kept to a slightly south-by-southeast heading to widen the distance between them and the Soviet shoreline. They slid past Vladivostok and made a good ten miles beyond the harbor mouth before static crackled over the international maritime frequency and a harsh voice demanded in Russian that they identify the vessel and return to port for clearance papers. The junk continued without responding. To the Penetrator's surprise, neither a high-speed patrol boat nor interceptors were scrambled to locate them. They now paralleled the North Korean coast and by mid-afternoon were well on the way to their original destination.

Two hours after darkness fell, the chugging marine diesel of the *Kaki Kara* ceased to labor and the small junk coasted in close to the black outline of land. The Penetrator, Kim Suŏng Ree, and their equipment waited on deck.

"We'll put you ashore here," Captain Heida whispered to the Penetrator. You should be a mile and a half north of the village. Once you leave my ship, there will be no further contact. Baldwin-*san* has agreed to that."

"Thank you, Captain Heida. It's been a little hairy, but overall a successful voyage."

"Hairy?" the Japanese skipper asked in puzzled confusion.

"An expression. Most nervous-making."

"Aah, so-o-o."

"You gotta be kiddin'," Kim chimed in. "I thought only Chinese actors playing Japanese soldiers in old Yankee propaganda films said that."

Captain Heida shot Kim a pained glance, then extended his hand in the darkness. "Good luck—to both of you."

A brief five-minute struggle with the surf put Mark and Kim ashore. They deflated the rubber raft and buried it in a thatch of saltbush undergrowth. They then hiked a quarter mile due west before the Penetrator called a halt and broke out his map. He used a converted penlight that featured a low level intensity LED (Light Emitting Diode) crystal instead of a bulb to check their location, orienting them with his compass. Satisfied, he directed Kim to follow him south.

When the Penetrator estimated they had reached a point half a mile from the village of

Kosŏng, he once more settled in under shelter of a large tree. He drew Kim close to him and whispered in the young Korean's ear.

"From here on it's up to you. Go in the village and get the general layout. Keep alert for anything that might help us. In particular any news about foreign children that might have been seen in the area."

"Gotcha. Meanwhile you get to stack 'Z's' and recover from the hassle we've been through." Kim spoke without rancor.

"No. I sit here, bite my nails, and worry like hell."

"You're some kind of guy, Greg," the Korean responded a moment before he slid off into darkness.

The Penetrator's assessment of how he would spend time came closer to truth than jest. While first one, then two hours passed, he found himself consumed with a sense of helplessness entirely alien to his makeup. He was the one to be out doing, the guy who handled the tough jobs. Sitting and waiting weren't a part of his programed responses. He tried to scan in his mind the memorized map of the narrow strip of land in which the kiddie killers had to be waiting to infiltrate the DMZ. Would an actual invasion be launched to support them?

He had no way of knowing. Too many factors remained undisclosed. He had to have some better intelligence than he'd been getting so far. With any luck, Kim might pick up something that would put them on the right trail. A longshot, considering his certainty that the numbers ran against them.

"Have I got news for you," Kim exulted when he

slid quietly out of the brush and sat down beside the Penetrator.

He gratefully leaned his tired back against the tree trunk.

"Give."

"There's a big shot from Pyongyang staying at the hotel. Only one in town and a dump, but he's got the royal suite. He's with the intelligence service and came down, according to a talkative bartender in the saloon next door, with another high mucky-muck, a certain Colonel Kum Lok Gee."

"I don't like it. It's too easy, too pat. It could be a diversion," the Penetrator speculated aloud.

"There's only one way to find out."

"Yeah. We have to go in there, take this wheel out, and question him."

# 14

## *TERMINAL INTERROGATION*

Major Huan Meng Tok of the National Security Force, North Korea's intelligence service, had spent a bad night. Restless, he had sat in his hotel room and reviewed the astounding documents given him by Colonel Kum Lok Gee. Preposterous! He tossed the thought aside as he had done the papers after an hour's study.

To use Occidental children against U.S. and Korean troops as squads of suicide terrorists sounded like the ravings of a drunk. Or a lunatic. Yet, the central government at Pyongyang had approved the plan. They had the backing of this strange organization, the SIE. Huan had protested the idea. When he saw that course to be useless, he had argued that the armed forces could never be mobilized and in position to support such an action by invasion in less than a month.

"You don't have a month," Colonel Gee had bellowed, leaning close to shout in Major Tok's face. "You have less than a week. The army is already on the move to the DMZ. The first contingents of troops arrive day after tomorrow. Tanks, artillery, infantry. More troops to follow. In four days the programed youngsters will be released, and within forty-eight hours the invasion shall unalterably be in motion."

Six days to cataclysm! Huan recoiled from the thought in stunned disbelief. Why had he not been informed? Colonel Gee had the answer. "You are a sector commander in internal security. You had no need to know regarding this until the time came to strike. Your military record is excellent and your reputation admirable. I personally asked for you to be in charge of internal security in the staging area. Now you have your orders and you will obey them."

Recalling the conversation, Major Tok glanced apprehensively at the photographs of his wife and children, in the metal-bound folding case he carried with him wherever he went. What would happen to them if the Americans came again like they had in 1951, with their guns and tanks and mortars, their shrieking jets with bombs and— napalm? He shuddered at the thought. Too much, too fast.

Until three days ago he had been a contented, if a bit complacent, bureaucrat in the central office of the security service in Pyongyang, in charge of evaluating reports sent in from agents of the internal security force in the far northern province of Chongjin. Twice a year, for week-long tours he visited the province for which he had responsibility. The rest of the time he spent with his lovely wife and beautiful youngsters. Now his comfortable world had been upended.

Because one group of Westerners wanted to

gain power over a large number of their fellow Occidentals, this unbelievable plot had been hatched and foisted off on his government. Murderous children running loose among the American troops soon to be massed right on the DMZ. What was to say they wouldn't turn their homicidal talents against North Korean soldiers? He had briefly met the *huasin*—the chinese word for the white-skinned barbarians seemed so much more suited to him than the Korean term—Dr. Treavor DiFalco in the capital.

The SIE psychologist had assured him and the other ranking officers assembled for the briefing that the children were all highly motivated to kill American soldiers. They could not be stopped from their task once the coded command had been given. They would also attack South Korean troops. Could they tell one Korean from another?

DiFalco had assured the assembled officers that once the invasion force crossed into South Korea, most of the children would have been exterminated or interned by the enemy and that those same troops would be completely demoralized by what they had been forced to do. No potential harm to North Korean personnel was anticipated. Further, DiFalo claimed, the American presence would be reduced to a few hard-core professionals who would not desert in the face of the horror of warring on innocent-looking youngsters, but who would not number sufficiently to slow down the drive on the southern capital at Seoul. Major Tok still had his reservations, though events passed a man too quickly in the modern world. No matter, he would cope. Although sleep continued to elude him until midnight came and went, he poured himself a large beaker of tea and dismissed his aide and two guards.

Major Tok removed his uniform and slid his thick, muscular legs into the soothing comfort of a pair of silk pajamas. The criminally un-Marxist bed wear had been a gift from his wife. With a grunt, Major Tok resigned himself to the merciless arms of insomnia. Whatever the outcome of the next few days, he would try to rejoin his family and together they would endure.

Kim led the Penetrator up the darkened back stairs of the rickety building that housed the hotel. The absence of visible guards near the alleged important official's room made Mark suspect the possibility of a trap, though he kept his thoughts to himself. They tiptoed down the hall and stopped outside Major Tok's room.

Before they had entered town, Mark and Kim had each slipped a *makoca,* a typical outer coat worn by Korean men, on over their nondescript Korean-made clothing. Kim reached under his and drew a silencer-equipped Stechkin, a Soviet-made 9mm machine pistol. Then he eased open the door and entered. Major Tok laid aside the book he had been trying to read and peered at the unannounced visitor.

"What is the meaning of this?"

Kim gestured with the Russian automatic weapon in his right hand. "You are coming with me, major."

"*Kkattak swu*—a risky measure. My men are quartered on this floor and the one below. One yell from me and you will be my prisoner."

"I think not. Put on some clothes and be quiet

about it or the first five rounds from this Stechkin will cut you in half—and no one will hear a shot fired."

"Are you from the reactionary resistance movement? Oh, we know all about you. Running-dog lackeys of the imperialist warmongers to the south."

Tension had begun to take a harsh drain on Kim's reserves. His voice crackled with but barely suppressed anger. "Save your Marxist rhetoric for your comrades in Pyongyang, you prick. Just do as I say and you'll stay alive." Kim stepped to the door and opened it. He motioned to the Penetrator.

Mark Hardin entered the room. He held his old standby, a Mark IV Sidewinder submachine gun, fitted with a bulky MAC silencer. Kim gave him an inquiring glance.

"Do we do it here?"

"Too much risk. We'll take him with us."

"How?" Kim asked.

The Penetrator bent and removed a small kit from where it was attached to his ankle by a Velcro strip. From it, he took a hypodermic needle and a vial of colorless liquid. "I'll put him to sleep. A light dose so we can get to the questions right away."

"You're speaking English," Huan accused the Korean while he shrugged into his shirt. "Mongrel batards of the CIA."

"Tell him how wrong his is," the Penetrator instructed.

While Major Tok focused his attention on Kim, the Penetrator stepped in close and injected the knockout drug into the major's exposed forearm.

In a clutch of seconds, the Korean intelligence chief slumped back onto his bed. The Penetrator released the Sidewinder and shoved it under his own *makoca* to let it hang by its sling. He muscled Tok over his shoulder in a fireman carry and walked to the door.

Surprisingly their hasty plan went undiscovered. Kim led the way down to the back entrance and they slipped out into the night. The village slept while they hurried Major Tok through the alleyways to the edge of Kosŏng and out into the rugged hills. The Penetrator gave Tok a counter-acting drug and waited fifteen minutes while the man came around.

"Okay, ask him about the kids. Have they been here? Does he even know about them?"

Kim repeated the question in Korean.

Major Tok couldn't believe what he heard. These agents, obviously CIA, he assured himself, knew about the plan to use children in an inva-sion of the South. He remained silent. The big man, the Occidental, slapped him with a solid, back-hand blow. Huan disassociated himself from pain—present or future—and stoically remained mute.

"Tell him we can do it easy or hard. With silenc-ers and a gag in his mouth, no one would hear a thing when I started shooting him in the ankles, knees, elbows—all of that."

Huan listened and still refrained from speaking.

"Okay, turkey, we do it with babble juice," the Penetrator advised. He opened his drug kit again and selected a blue-capped vial. He judged Major Tok's weight at around a hundred thirty. He carefully drew the dosage of sodium pentothal and injected it. When the powerful substance had its effect, the Penetrator began questioning again. He soon got past the preliminaries.

"Are the children here or close to here?"

"Yes. In three camps along the demarcation."

"What cover is being used for the local population?"

"*Kakyo,*" Major Tok began in sleepy-voiced Korean, then went on for a second.

"He says they are supposed to be European children from a Communist Youth Organization, here to do bridge building."

"Where?"

"*Nāpyen?*" Kim demanded.

"*Nāpyen kāto Kosŏng-Pokkye-ri kalangi cita ta kalam Puche, taka suta taliq mak katay.*"

"He says, 'Where the Kosŏng-Pokkye-ri highway divides into two branches you come up to a Buddhist temple. Beyond that there is a path to a premises.' *Katay?*"

"*Hē. Katay-katay.*"

"Oh, a house and lot. Large I gather."

"The children are all there?"

Huan Tok murmured on for several seconds in a slack-tongued voice. Kim translated. "He says that the men who are in charge stay there. Also some of the children."

"How long will they be there?"

In reply, Major Tok spat a single word, the effect of the truth drug apparently wearing off. "*Natal.*"

"About four days."

"Where are the others kept?"

Kim asked, Huan refused to answer. Kim tried again.

Huan Tok managed to work up a gob of saliva

and spit on the South Korean's trousers. The Penetrator rose and swung the silenced muzzle of the Sidewinder in line with Huan's forehead.

"We've gotten all we can from him. At least it's a start. Like dominoes—first one, then the next, and the next. We'll get them all."

Suddenly clarity drove through the drug hangover that assaulted Huan's mind. He saw Old Man Death hovering near at hand, one boney hand beckoning. Thoughts of his children, the possibility of imminent war, his beautiful, desirable wife flashed through his overwhelming terror. Of a sudden, loyalty to his job and the party didn't seem all that important. He wanted so badly to live. Groveling on his knees, Huan clasped his hands together and begged in a cracked, whining voice.

*Kātay! Kātay! Taka suta nalak!"*

"He's begging for mercy. He says he's coming nearer to hell."

The Penetrator smiled grimly. "Tell him he's right."

Mark tightened his finger on the three-stage progressive trigger of the Sidewinder. The compact submachine gun softly chuffed once and a fat .45 slug bashed its way through Huan Tok's forehead.

It mercifully disconnected enough nerve centers so that Major Tok didn't experience the agony of his body while his spirit slipped into the eternal midnight of death.

"Let's head for that Buddhist temple," the Penetrator commanded.

# 15

## *MOUNTAIN ENCAMPMENT*

To the north of Kosong, the rolling hills of the coastal plain quickly turned into the stark, rugged mountains of Korea, so often and accurately compared to the bleak Laguna Mountains of Southern California. The terrain lacked only the lovely, white, waxlike flowers of the yucca and palm trees scattered on the lower slopes to make the similarity complete. Unfortunately, the howling blizzards and subzero temperatures of Arctic winters made this clime inhospitable to such flora. Cacti existed, though, as the Penetrator soon discovered.

"Ouch. Damnit, there aren't this many cacti in Arizona."

"Perhaps we should have waited for daylight," Kim suggested through lips quirked at the corners into a half-smile. "Moving around in the dark in Korea is an acquired art. It requires a smooth, sweeping stride quite unlike that used in jungle or on a desert."

"Write it up for the Sierra Club magazine, Kim." Mark changed the subject. "I figure we've circled far enough to avoid any patrols that might be out.

We should be in position by sunrise to observe the camp."

"What do we do from there?"

"From what I've discovered so far, the programing of these kids has followed a standard system. Otherwise they'd be uncontrollable, kill anyone they came upon. So, we have to terminate the people who control them and also destroy all records and training plans so that no one else can activate the killing instinct implanted in the children."

"You don't want much. Okay, so we first get the lay of the camp and then move in. How do we deal with the kids?"

The Penetrator's grim features could not be seen in the predawn blackness. "I'm opposed to killing them. They're as much victims as the troops they're programed to assassinate. If we're smart enough, and quiet enough, we can get in, hit any of the instructors who are there, and be out of the camp before the youngsters know what happened."

Kim grunted in doubt of success along those lines. He checked the time on his wristwatch and adjusted the straps of the small backpack he wore. "We'd better get going, then. The sun comes up without much warning around here."

Dr. Treavor DiFalco sat on the small side porch of the house he used as headquarters and sipped at his evening coffee. He listened to the slight pattering sounds made by tiny bodies hurtling against the screens that surrounded the verandah. How could a country that got so cold in winter have so many insects? The small creatures tried vainly to get at the irresistible lure of a whitely glowing gasoline lantern that sat on a table next to DiFalco. By its light he tried to read Vidal's *Julian*. He needed the diversion, for the day had gone badly.

His charges had started to grow restless and intractable. Like every day since their arrival, morning and afternoon had been devoted to training in the use of firearms and hand grenades and special instruction in constructing booby-traps. There had been a near accident that could have claimed half a dozen lives. Quick, competent action by one of the North Korean sergeants, an expert in demolitions, had prevented tragedy. The term suited, DiFalco acknowledged, because he had been standing within three feet of the deadly, but improperly assembled, bomb. He felt that he could not endure any more incidents like that. Why had his superiors in the society put him on this project in the first place?

He had never kept it a secret that he held his fellow man in utter contempt. The study of psychology had transformed his vague dislikes into cold, but irrational, hatred, because through it he began to recognize in himself the same attributes he so despised in others. For years, since his collegiate days, this had provided a focus for his feelings of inferiority and rejection.

His father had deserted the family when Treavor was nine. His mother took a succession of lovers, none of whom had any affection to expend on five children under the age of twelve. Money had never been a problem, yet it never seemed to buy him friendship. Treavor DiFalco learned early to internalize his emotions, to carry grudges. One

day, he promised himself, he would get even.
Later, through the revelations he experienced in
his psych courses, he became able to verbalize
his scorn.

"Man," he would frequently expound to his circle of liberal, protorevolutionary contemporaries
at Boston University. "What a disgusting animal.
He has tainted the air, soiled the water, sterilized
the land with harsh chemicals, and slaughtered
the innocent wildlife for his sport. And, worst pollu-
tion of all, he spawns like maggots and sends
these mindless, wriggling white forms out to insure
ultimate chaos by overpopulation. Can anyone
cite a better example of compounding a felony?"

Rarely did he find a challenger to his rhetoric.

His reflections on those halcyon days suddenly
presented him with a new truth. Of all the misera-
ble buffoons that comprised mankind, the North
Koreans had to be the biggest cosmic joke. They
had no chance to win a conflict such as the one
devised to employ the orphan children. Yet they
leaped at the opportunity to strike at their cousins
to the south. How could they hope to oppose the
modern technology of the United States—whether
in the hands of Americans or South Koreans?

Given all the advantages of a progressive,
Marxist state, still, after thirty years they wallowed
in the stasis of a barbaric, feudal society. No matter, though, he reasoned. Their little brushfire war
would aid the goals of the society and that was
what counted. Another Vietnam-style encounter
would enrich everyone in the society and further
weaken the decadent American populace. Perhaps Gore Sasson had been right, DiFalco
thought. The impending skirmish might rob the

people in the States of their last erg of will to resist. Then the society would have it all. Ah, idle speculation led to sloppy thinking, he chided himself. Dr. DiFalco put his book aside and rose to extinguish the lantern.

He froze at the sound of rustling in the bushes outside the little house. Two long seconds passed and no other disturbance came. Perhaps one of the guards checking on the house, he dismissed. He reached for the regulator knob, then looked up, startled, when the screen door creaked open. Standing before him was a cruel-looking, tall, powerful man who pointed the muzzle of a silenced automatic weapon at Dr. DiFalco's middle.

Throughout the day the Penetrator and Kim had kept watch on the camp of apprentice murderers. The children had been drilled in the use of firearms and grenades, while a constant barrage of sound washed over them.

Hard-rock music blared from speakers wired into the trees, each familiar tune followed by a variety of songs specially written for the SIE which extolled the virtues of one-world government, or of defeat and destruction of Yankee imperialist forces on foreign soil, or held out promise of a new world order run by the young, for the benefit of only the young. It all had an effect, the Penetrator saw, as innocent youthful faces suffused with kill lust. When at last the call for the evening meal came, Mark and Kim began to lay out their plans.

Kim would handle outside security while the Penetrator went after DiFalco and the records.

Their careful examination of the campsite, and the house in particular, had revealed that only Treavor DiFalco, of all the SIE leaders, was present. Once Mark had the documents, he would kill DiFalco and they would withdraw, hopefully without alarming the camp or guards. So far, it had gone well, the Penetrator felt while he studied the immobilized man in front of him.

"Dr. DiFalco, I have some questions to ask you."

"Who are you?" DiFalco demanded, although his quick glance at the high cheekbones, hawk nose, and snapping black eyes left him no doubt that his enemy was the Penetrator.

"No time for introductions. Where do you keep the records on this bizarre experiment of yours?"

"You're insane. All I have to do is call out. This camp is well guarded, you'll never get away."

"We got in here, didn't we? I want those papers, DiFalco, or I start blowing little chunks off of you."

Dr. DiFalco had not moved since the Penetrator entered, his hand still poised beside the gasoline lantern. In the presence of the threat, he made sure to remain entirely motionless. From outside came the fluttering burp of a silenced machine pistol. A man screamed and lights flared on in the compound. A siren began to wail.

"Oh, shit! We're in for it now," Kim yelled as he rushed up the steps.

In the same instant Dr. DiFalco saw possible reprieve. He seized the lantern and threw it at the Penetrator. Then he dived through the open doorway to the house.

The Penetrator's three-round burst from the Sidewinder came a fraction of a second too late. He had lashed out with his left forearm to deflect the lantern and thrown off his timing. The slugs chewed wood from the doorframe while the lamp smashed into a porch post and crashed to the floor.

White gas spilled from the reservoir and ignited on the still-glowing mantles. Flames began to eat into the floorboards.

"He went in there," the Penetrator told Kim. They crossed to the door at oblique angles to keep out of any possible line of fire. Kim poked the bulbous muzzle of the Stechkin around the jam and squeezed off a rapid five rounds.

A yelp of pain came from inside and then a flashlight flared to life. Two muscular youths in the pajamalike fatigue uniform of the North Korean Army came charging down the short hall, each one clutching an AK-74 assault rifle, the new Soviet weapon in 5.56mm. Artifically induced fanaticism twisted their faces into masks of rage and the flash hiders on their pieces spat thin laces of flame while streams of .223 hornets buzzed through the air. The simple demands of survival solved the Penetrator's dilemna over shooting the youngsters.

A pair of silent, deadly bursts of .45 slugs knocked the teenaged killers off their feet. Their tangled bodies tripped up the next one to come forth to die for his puppet master. Kim lobbed a grenade down the hall and entered with a rush alongside the Penetrator.

Behind them the fire spread rapidly and ahead the dark house beckoned to suicide. Mark and Kim made a cautious check of the rooms along their way, found them to be empty. Then they came to one that had been locked from inside.

"You want to flip for who goes through this one first?" Kim asked laconically.

"We're running out of time." From his pocket, the Penetrator took a quarter-pound block of C-4 explosive. He used his sleeve knife to cut a one-ounce cube from the pliable material. He molded the C-4 around the doorknob and pressed a fuse cap into the plastic. He crimped a length of black, waterproof dynamite fuse into the open end of the detonating device and lit the frayed end. It sputtered to smoky life. Mark and Kim retreated down the hall and into rooms.

The blast, sharp and powerful, raised clouds of dust throughout the building. It temporarily blew out the flames on the porch and reduced the door to flying splinters. Only the back edge remained, attached to warped hinges. Before the enemy could recover, the Penetrator·and Kim charged DiFalco's office.

Two Korean guards died, one to a ripping blast from Kim's Stechkin 9mm machine pistol and the other to a single shot from Mark's Sidewinder. Treavor DiFalco, covered by debris from the explosion, cowered behind a desk. On it sat a large briefcase, partly filled with files and loose papers. The Penetrator walked menacingly toward the thoroughly demoralized SIE operative.

"Where are the other children, DiFalco?"

"I—I don't know for sure. I mean, I know where some of them are. They're with Gore Sasson. If—if you let me live, I'll tell you—" DiFalco waited with trepidation through the Penetrator's purposeful silence. "The camp is located some thirty kilometers north of Pokkye-ri and closer to the DMZ than this is."

"How many?"

"A hundred, hundred and twenty. The rest are with Colonel Gee of North Korean intelligence, but I don't know where." DiFalco swallowed, trying to ease his fear-dry throat. "Y-you are going to let me live, aren't you? I can make it well worth your while. I have money, power, influence back in the States."

"This is a war, DiFalco. There are bound to be some casualties." The Penetrator shot the SIE agent in the chest. He took a small thermite grenade from his coat pocket, pulled the pin, and dropped it into DeFalco's briefcase.

"Aren't you going to take those papers back to Washington for study first?" Kim asked, incredulous.

"Hell no. I don't even want our side to have the ability to do something like this. Now, let's find a way to get out of here."

Bullets tore through the thin outer walls of the house and forced the Penetrator and Kim to crawl along the hallway to escape their fatal kiss. The corridor, shaped like a *T* with the long crossarm running from front to rear and a short base that led to the side porch, gave access to a variety of rooms, two of which had the traditional *shoji* screen walls and sliding door of lacquered rice paper. The Penetrator entered the first one he came to and studied the layout for a moment. Then he motioned Kim to follow.

"The power plant should be right outside this

wall of the building." Mark slid open a narrow window and peered outside.

North Korean guards ran in all directions. Some seemed occupied with containing the children in their barracks buildings, while others fought the rekindled blaze at the side of the house and a few fired their weapons toward the location of Treavor DiFalco's office, where the exploded thermite had ignited another hotly raging conflagration. He spotted the low generator shed a yard to his right and only inches short of twenty feet from the house. The Penetrator took a grenade from his belt, armed it, and tossed it through the open end of the shack.

*Krangggl*

The grenade did its work of wrecking the generator. Instantly the powerful yard lights flickered and went out. Mark and Kim hurried to the opposite side of the house as the guards, alerted to this new threat, rushed to the scene of devastation. Quietly they slipped out an open window and waited tensely to determine that no hidden menace lurked nearby.

Satisfied, the Penetrator tugged on Kim's coat sleeve and indicated the direction they would take. Mark started off on silent feet, eyes casting about the darkness for any threat. Off to the right the low Korean brush wavered in green-black solidity, reflecting the light from the porch fire. In the other direction excited voices called to each other in Korean and English. In the confusion they covered fifty yards of open ground without even a challenge.

"You there," came a sudden peremptory voice

from behind Mark and Kim. "Where are you going?"

"We thought we saw someone running off into the bushes," Kim responded in Korean.

"All right, then. Check it out. If you make contact, one man stay with the enemy, send the other back for reinforcements."

"Yes, sergeant," Kim repled.

A dozen jogging strides brought the Penetrator and Kim into the security of dense brush and low trees. They worked their way through the chaparral for a quarter mile, then Mark called a halt.

"I thought we were in for a firefight back there."

"These *makoca* coats provided enough protective coloration in the dark," Kim opined.

"Good thing too. Next stop Professor Gore Sasson's murder school."

# 16

## SEARCH AND DESTROY

Half an hour of hard going brought the Penetrator and Kim back to the clear road heading west. Before going on, Kim called a brief halt. In the cover of a small copse of trees, he dragged from his pack a compact, short-range radio transmitter. He climbed a tree and strung out the antenna.

"What's all this about?" the Penetrator inquired.

"What Major Tok said about a resistance movement wasn't Communist bullshit. There really is one. I'm going to try to make contact and have the local cell move in to see nothing happens to those kids until we can work something out to get them over to the other side."

"Good thinking. I like it. Was this Toro's idea?"

"Not exactly," Kim hedged.

"Who else do you work for besides Baldwin?"

"I'd rather not say. As it stands, I don't know anything about you and vice versa."

"I'll buy that. Get on the horn and let's see about some sort of transportation. This 'highway' as Tok called it isn't much more than a goat trail and we've got a long distance to cover."

"Unless you want to take on the army, the best we can hope for will be a couple of bicycles."

"I'd settle for a skateboard right now," the Penetrator concluded. "We might as well eat now and save time later."

"Right. You cook, I'll play radioman."

"Have some more of that brandy, Loren," Gore Sasson urged the seveteen-year-old fanatic who had done a lot to whip into line the contingent of children in this camp.

Loren Chase helped himself to a generous quantity of the Hennessy Five Star and returned to his chair. He and Sasson relaxed in a second-floor room of a stout stone farmhouse located one mile north of the DMZ. The comforts provided by the North Korean government, although not luxurious, allowed them an adequate existence. Chase looked atentively at the older man when Sasson began to speak again.

"You know, Loren, I find your company quite refreshing compared to those—those little monsters out there." Loren Chase raised a quizzical eyebrow. "You have a solid grasp of what the SIE commitment to this project is. For my own part, though I understand their reasoning, I find it unrealistic. Who gives a damn about North Korea? Do you? Does anyone?

"I hate Korea, the Koreans, children in general, and most of all, I despise the idea of actually exposing myself in what can be nothing short of a combat situation. I have too much to offer to the society to have my brains scattered on some battlefield for a mob of Oriental Communists.

"I've confided a great deal to you, Loren, and you are aware of how the society has long been using Communism as well as our people inside various governments, the media, and entertainment to slant opinion toward the Corporate World Authority. Being among the informed, the insiders so to speak, do you see why there is no contradiction in my dislike and contempt for Communists and our using them to achieve our goals?"

"Yes, sir. From the books you've given me to read, I gather that twentieth-century Communism was created as a front by the same people who organized the SIE."

"Precisely. It has an appeal among persons who have never known freedom. All the high-flown phrases of Marxism provide scant nourishment to the intellect. They are pitched on the gut level. 'Workers of the world unite!' So stirring on the visceral plain, yet not even original when Marx wrote the words in the last century. The same mindless exhortation was used by Catalinus two thousand years ago to stir up the guttersnipe rabble of Rome."

"That only shows that most persons react on the gut level, as you call it. Thus, when they actually embrace Communism, you lose your respect for them."

"Precisely, my boy. You are a marvel. So here we sit in the middle of a primitive country with a flock of mindwarped children, waiting to unleash the little hellions on their fellow countrymen and Korean allies while we're not even sure the North Korean army can get into position in time to capitalize on the diversion created by these brats."

"What did you propose as an alternative, sir? I'm sure this conversation has been leading to that conclusion."

"Indeed it has. Brilliant observation, Loren. I presented an immediate and far more beneficial project. The *Séparatiste* movement, Loren my boy. That's where the society's greatest chance of success lies. Why, had they directed this little experiment in mind control and terrorist tactics toward Quebec, we would soon have a base of operations with immediate access to the United States and all the protections of a recognized, independent nation with its own language and laws."

Loren Chase mulled over the professor's words. He didn't know much about the French-Canadian situation, didn't care much either. For his mentor's sake, he pulled a sincere face.

"An interesting concept, sir. I can see where it would be of benefit to the society to completely control a country of its own." He glanced at a small porcelain clock on an antique lacquer table. "I would be interested in hearing more about it, but it is getting late and there is another day of training."

"Ah, yes. Tomorrow. And then another dawn, when we shall discover if all this be folly or fortune."

An hour before sunrise the Penetrator and Kim crouched in the brush at the edge of a large clearing. Mark pointed to his left, made a sweeping gesture with his arm.

"You go around that way, take out the guards when you encounter them. I'll go the other and when we meet over by that large stone building we'll move in on the camp."

"Do we terminate the guards?"

"Not unless it can't be avoided."

With a nod of ascent, Kim faded into the undergrowth. The Penetrator took Ava from his backpack and checked the magazine to make sure knockout rounds had been loaded. Then he started on his task. Kim would have the harder job disabling the guards barehanded, and they could have worked together, though for personal security reasons, Mark didn't want the clever Korean to know about his gas-powered dart gun. A hundred yards to his right he came upon the first sentry.

Ava hissed and the Penetrator rushed forward to catch the convulsing man and ease him to the ground so his thrashing would not alert others. When the drugged sentinel lay still, the Penetrator edged on to the next outpost.

Two men crouched under a tree, talking softly and smoking, in violation of every regulation for guard duty. Long hours and the security of being in one's own country had undermined the Korean soldiers' training. Mark fired a dart, took aim, and released a second one.

"Saaagggh!" The first sentry uttered a strangled cry and went into nearly instant convulsions. The second Korean leaped to his feet. The dart intended to render him unconscious had gone low and lodged in the thick padding of his coat, which kept the needle from entering flesh.

With no time for a second aimed shot, the Pentrator dashed in and drove the soldier off his feet with a *mae geri keage* front snap kick to the right kidney. The force of the blow drove the air from the Korean's lungs and deprived him of a chance to yell a warning. The Penetrator dropped onto his victim and shoved his head forward. The blade of Mark's Enos-designed sleeve knife came into the open and he forced it into the feebly struggling man's occipital foramen and slashed from side to side to sever the spinal cord at the base of the medulla. The Penetrator withdrew the bloodsmeared weapon, wiped it clean on the Korean's *makoca,* and returned it to its forearm sheath. Quietly he headed toward the next post.

Fifteen minutes later, with the light of false dawn glowing over the eastern hills, the Penetrator linked up with Kim. The young South Korean nursed a slight wound in his left shoulder.

"You sure believe in doing things the hard way," Kim muttered. "There'll be guards at the headquarters building."

"I know it. I brought along an AK and two pistol belts."

"How about that? So did I. And a couple of caps."

"If our Korean clothing will pass, we've got it wired then. At least until we can get in close enough to take out the sentries." The Penetrator helped Kim tie a compress over his wound and the Korean shrugged back into his *makoca.* "Now's as good a time as any."

"You two! Get back to your posts," a burly guard at the door to the stone house challenged when the Penetrator and Kim walked out of the trees and approached. "You're not relieved yet."

"A message for Mr. Sasson," Kim responded.

"It takes two of you to deliver it?" the sergeant's caustic tone reflected the tribulations of noncommissioned officers in every army.

"He's the mesenger," Kim countered, hooking a thumb over his shoulder toward Mark, who walked a bit behind to hide his features.

"All right, you've done your job, now get back on guard."

Kim replied with a *shuto* stroke to the sergeant's throat. The North Korean soldier gulped in the last air he would ever breathe. His larynx collapsed under the force of Kim's strike and he began to crumple before Kim finished with a *gyaku shuto* reverse chop to the nerve ganglion at the base of the sergeant's neck. The dying man dropped to his knees. Immediately two more guards rushed forward.

The Penetrator engaged the first one. He pivoted away inside a bayonet thrust and aimed a *yoko hiji ate* side elbow strike at the man's unprotected head. The North Korean jerked his helmeted skull away to avoid the blow, then swung his rifle in an attempt to smash into Mark's ribs. The Penetrator avoided it easily and slashed downward with a *shuto uchi* chop that numbed the man's left arm. The rifle clattered from his grasp. Immediately he assumed a *tae kwan do* defensive position, similar to the *soto hachiji dachi* of *shito-ryu* karate.

From that posture he launched a low kick.

The Penetrator stopped it with a *sukui uki* sweeping block that resulted in Mark grasping his opponent at the ankle and slightly above the knee. He heaved backward.

The soldier hit the ground.

The force of the landing drove the breath from the Korean's lungs and his head cracked painfully against the hard soil. To his left Mark saw Kim finish his attacker with a double *oyayubi ippon ken* thumb knuckle blow to both ears and a *seiken* forefist punch to the diaphragm. No other challenge came at them.

"Let's get inside," the Penetrator suggested.

"What was that noise outsi—" A corporal in the green-brown uniform of the North Korean army broke off his question when he looked up from behind a small desk in the entryway and saw two grim-faced, armed men confronting him. The Penetrator bashed him into unconsciousness with a butt stroke from the AK-74 he carried. He abandoned the Soviet assault rifle and brought out his Sidewinder, then he and Kim hurried to the stairway.

"Sasson will have his quarters on the second floor," the Penetrator announced with certainty.

At the top of the stairs, the Penetrator glimpsed an unbelievable sight. Two Korean guards, who should have no doubt been patrolling the upper hallway, sat in the center of the corridor floor, drinking from a large flask of *Tsing-tao* Communist Chinese beer and playing cards. The Penetrator climbed the final steps and sent them off to poker players' paradise with two short, silent bursts from his Sidewinder.

One soldier lived long enough to cry out in his death agony. Immediately a door flung open and the Penetrator saw an even more ludicrously incredible spectacle. Loren Chase, totally naked, his curly auburn locks in wild disarray, stood in the doorway, clutching a Kalashnikov 5.56mm assault rifle.

"You bastards!" Loren screamed and tried to bring the AK-74 to bear.

The Penetrator saw death coming his way and, with no other choice, squeezed off a three-round burst that pulped Loren's lungs and drove the boy back into his room, where he died a lonely and inglorious death for the Cause. Mark motioned to Kim and spoked quickly, quietly.

"Go down to the office. Find all the papers on the project and destroy them. I'll take care of Sasson."

Kim, for not the first time, looked dubious. "Are you sure you have the authority to destroy all the evidence and waste these guys?"

"It came from 'the highest source in Washington,' fella. You want to argue with that?"

Kim thought of the man who lived at 1600 Pennsylvania Avenue and swallowed hard. "Christ, no."

"Then get on with it." The Penetrator turned away before Kim could make any reply and strode down the hall to the closed door a the end.

Gore Sasson, kneeling, cowered at the side of his bed. He threw the small pistol he clutched into plain sight at the center of the covers. "Don't shoot me. Who are you? What do you want?"

"Where is Gee and the rest of your murder-programed kids?"

"I—I'll tell you. They're between here and

Chŏrwŏn, on Highway One at the DMZ. The camp is three kilometers outside the city, right on the edge of the dead zone."

"Okay. What's the reason behind the SIE's involvement?"

"I won't—I can't tell you that. If I do, they'll have me killed."

The Penetrator grinned wickedly a Gore Sasson, assuming his best "tough guy" scowl. "Then there's only one difference between the SIE goons and me. I'm right here in the room with you and I'll for sure kill you if you don't talk."

Sasson wiped his brow with a quaking hand. "A-all right. Anything. If you—if you mean it that you won't kill me if I tell you what I know."

"Let's start with who 'they' are."

"Well, t-the head of the society in the United States is David Felder. Then there's the Schwartzehelm banking family in Europe, ah, Prince Augie von Schwartzehelm and a lot of his cousins. Julius Glick in Geneva and Peter van der Moers in South Africa—he's into diamonds. Then there's Taiji Ozaka in Tokyo, he's in steel, coal, and oil and—and the only other member of the ruling circle that I personally know is Howard Loewn, who has interests in broadcasting and a film studio." Sasson's face, if possible, took on even more pallor.

"They are absolutely ruthless. If they ever learn I talked, they'll have me killed. There's no way to prove it, no tangible evidence, like always, but I'm convinced they ordered Walter Cottler removed. He knew too much."

"More than that, he was going to tell everyone

who listened to his radio programs and watched his TV commentaries. Yes. That much I had figured out. And, for what it's worth, I agree with you that it can never be proven. Tell me more about the North Korean thing and the kiddie killers."

"North Korea had been planning an invasion of the South since they'd been promised that U.S. troops would be withdrawn. We, the society that is, convinced the leaders to delay until we gave the word."

"What for?"

"To be able to obtain the greatest financial advantage, naturally. With our foreign and American manufactories, the society would be making a profit from both sides. Then Treavor DiFalco came up with this idea, about four years ago, of how we could further demoralize the American population and in paticular, American armed forces. He made a presentation to the ruling circle based on using children as a horror factor.

"From the first, I was opposed to it. The society should have devoted primary focus on securing the freedom of Quebec. This adventuring halfway round the world to aid an insig—"

"Let's get back to the children," the Penetrator cut him off. "How are they controlled? When will they be put to use?"

"They are to infiltrate South Korea starting at dawn tomorrow. Only Dr. DiFalco, Colonel Gee, and myself have the key to activate their conditioned responses. Except for a few who took to the Cause without excessive persuasion, who are on their own."

"Only the three of you?"

Sasson nodded. "Of course, anyone who had access to the case histories and the indoctrination scenario could quickly take charge."

"Dr. DiFalco's copy of the records has been disposed of and yours is being destroyed right now. That leaves only Colonel Gee."

"What do you mean?"

"DiFalco is dead and you are soon going to be."

"No, wait!" Gore Sasson cried when he saw the muzzle of the silenced submachine gun center on his hairless, pallid chest. "You—you promised me that if I cooperated, I'd not—"

"Sometimes I lie a little," the Penetrator said before he squeezed the trigger.

# 17
## RACING THE CLOCK

The Penetrator managed to remove a sidecar motorcycle from the small motorpool near the headquarters building. He and Kim kept alert to the constant possibility that their presence would be noted and an alarm given. They exercised cautious stealth to roll the small vehicle down a winding path in the forest until they reached the North Korean version of the South's Highway 1. All the way there, the Penetrator worked silently to reassure himself that he fought a war, or at the least what he did prevented a far bloodier conflict than any side desired.

In a final contact with Dan Griggs, prior to embarking from Japan on the *Kaki Kara Maru*, he had been told that the situation remained deadlocked. There would be no public disclosure of the role played by the SIE in the training of child assassins.

Despite this, Dan informed Mark, the 'highest source' in Washington felt that the leaders of the experiment were far too dangerous to be allowed to live. The conundrum was how to bring them to justice without publicity. Mark felt he had the answer. Yet, to coldly, dispassionately gun down a cowardly, cringing man like Gore Sasson weighed heavily on his conscience. He could look forward to many hours in the sweat lodge to expiate this burden, and that of the youngsters he'd had to kill, from his low self. His somber reflections ended when Kim climbed into the sidecar. Mark swung a leg over the saddle of the bike and cycled the kick-starter.

"Hang-on," he advised Kim. "This is going to be a wild ride. We have less than twenty-four hours to find and stop Colonel Gee."

"Children of the New World Order!" Dr. Treavor DiFalco's voice came from a tape recording being played for the formation of kiddie-killer squads standing in a clearing within eyesight of Allied troops across the DMZ, screened from view only by a thick stand of trees. The dead SIE member's words of praise rolled out to listeners totally unaware of his termination and the disruption of two-thirds of their force.

"You have accomplished a great deal toward the eventual liberation of the oppressed peoples of the world. Your excellence in training, loyalty, dedication to the Cause, and tireless enthusiasm through difficult situations mark you as examples for the others who will follow you to emulate. At last the classes and field exercises have come to an end.

"Tomorrow at dawn, you will put into practice the many skills you have acquired. You shall go forth to meet the enemy and you shall destroy him—without hesitation, without thought, without mercy. Honor shall cloak your shoulders and victory shall spring from your hands." The tape ended and Colonel Kum Lok Gee stepped forward, facing the civilian-clad youngsters.

"You have heard the words of your mentor, Dr. DiFalco. The tide of history is on our side. You shall play a most important part in forming the world that comes after today. Do not shirk your duty. Do not cringe from self-sacrifice for the good of the Cause. Kill! Kill! Kill!"

The children cheered as though at a football game. Colonel Gee gave them a smile of satisfaction and dismissed the formation. He strode to his office in the headquarters room and summoned his adjutant. When the North Korean captain entered, Gee spoke to him in a quiet voice, tinged with concern.

"We have not heard from DiFalco and Sasson for two days. If the infiltration is not coordinated, the young people will be discovered before they manage to insinuate themselves among the enemy troops.

"Worse, still," he added. "I have not heard from that incompetent, Tok. I have no idea of the status of our own troops, or even if the lead elements of the invasion will be here on time."

The captain looked surprised. "You mean you weren't told? A message came in while you were holding the morning formation. Major Tok disappeared three nights ago. No trace of him. Another man is being sent from Pyongyang to oversee troop movements and maintain security along the border—but—"

"I'll have the man's head who failed to tell me immediately. This might delay the operation and we can hold these children only so long or they will begin to deteriorate. They are at their peak now and we dare not delay for long." Gee thought a moment, then rose. "We will release them on schedule. At least that might stir faster action from those dolts in Pyongyang. See that arms and equipment are ready for issue by this evening." "Yes, sir."

At the outset of the journey southward toward Chŏrwŏn, the Penetrator and Kim had the advantage of darkness. Once the sun had risen, they relied upon the uniformlike appearance of their clothing and their visible weapons to discourage inquiry. They covered most of the fifty-mile trip without incident, until they came upon a military control point some ten miles from their objective.

The Penetrator slowed to a stop at the back of a line of farm carts and pedestrian traffic. Mark's quick mind soon devised a bold, if risky, plan. He turned his head to Kim and spoke in a whisper to avoid being overheard.

"Do you have any sort of papers along? Something typewritten if possible?"

"Sure," Kim responded. He dug into the confines of a flap pocket.

"Good. That'll do fine." The Penetrator pulled out of line onto the verge of the narrow road and explained his gambit to Kim while he drove toward the roadblock.

"Halt!" an elderly sergeant armed with an obsolete PPSh-41 Russian-made submachine gun called to them. The internal-security-branch check points such as this were run by old soldiers on the verge of retirement, and they were rarely armed with the more modern weapons available to the army.

"Official business," Kim told him in an arrogant tone. He waved the folded papers to emphasize his meaning.

"That does not mean you can jump ahead of the line, comrade."

"These are top priority. Messages on the invasion force moving down to the DMZ."

The sergeant scowled and hesitated a moment, then signaled for the barrier to be raised. "Pass on through, then. I hope we whip them this time!" he shouted, then grumbled into the exhaust of the rapidly departing motorcycle, "I remember the last war only too well."

Indications of a military build-up became clearer to the Penetrator the closer they came to Chŏrwŏn. Two miles north of the city, Mark turned the motorcycle off into a narrow side trail. From this point on, Mark knew, their search would be more a matter of chance than surety.

"Petey, do—do you really think what we're doin' is for the best?" Twelve-year-old Robbie Fenton poked his head over the side of his bunk in the barracks room at the encampment outside Chŏrwŏn. His inquisitive gray eyes peered hopefully at his friend and a lock of black hair fell across his high, fair-skinned forehead.

"Sure," Petey replied. His black eyes snapped with conviction and he shook his deeply russet curls in impatience. The thick mat of freckles on his face writhed with his effort to assure his friend.

"Do—" he began and hesitated, then thought out his approach.

"Do you really wanna kill 'merican soldiers an'—and maybe be killed yourself?"

"N-no, Petey. But—what about the Cause?"

"Remember back at the home? What Dennis said about the Cause only being another name for Communism? And that when the chance came, he was gonna run away? Well, that's what we're doin', gettin' away."

"Well—I guess you're right." Robbie climbed from his bunk and joined Petey on the cold floor. The boys quickly dressed, except for their shoes.

"Keep 'em off until we get to the trees," Petey advised, then tiptoed to the door.

Outside the youngsters paused a moment. "Which way's south?" Robbie inquired, peering at the cloud-scudded sky.

Petey studied the few visible constellations until he recognized the North Star. "Uh—that way." Robbie hesitated.

"C'mon, Robbie. It's our only chance. We go over to the other side, tell them the truth, and maybe—maybe they won't put us in jail."

Silently Petey and Robbie started off toward South Korea.

Only six hours remained, the Penetrator estimated, before the SIE would put its monstrous plan into operation. He lay beside Kim at the crest of a small ridge that overlooked Colonel Gee's camp. No sounds disturbed the silence and there appeared to be no guards moving around. Mark turned to Kim, who seemed to be focused on another world.

"The name of the game is to get in and out without being spotted and head for the DMZ."

Kim removed a small headset from his left ear and whispered to the Penetrator. "I got the signal. The partisans have started to move the children in the other camps toward the border." Then he acknowledged the Penetrator's observation. "Nice if we can pull it off. We haven't been that lucky so far."

"I don't see any sign of roving patrols, though we'd better circle the camp first to make sure. Then head for that bunker. From the looks of it, that's Gee's headquarters."

"Right. See you in about forty-five minutes."

"Make it an hour and let's be positive," the Penetrator advised. "Good luck."

Halfway around his semicircular course, the Penetrator encountered a guard post. Unlike the previous encampments, the sentries turned out not to be North Korean soldiers, but youngsters from the SIE murder brigade. The Penetrator briefly faced a dilemma. He could dart one with Ava, only that would doubtless mean the second boy would have to die. He could also kill them both. Neither solution satisfied him. He decided to watch for a while. He had plenty of time.

Ten minutes later he made his decision. The boys moved about restlessly, bored and obviously indifferent to their duties. They lacked combat-wise experience to guide them in their actions. If their carelessness extended to other situations, his plan might work. The Penetrator dropped onto his belly and crawled to a position that placed him between the guard post and the camp. Then he thrashed the bushes a little and called out in the highest pitched voice he could muster.

"Hey, man, it's cold enough out here to freeze your balls off."

"No shit," a thirteen-year-old called in a soprano register from the machine-gun nest. "You bring us some coffee?"

The Penetrator had moved closer and spoke in his own voice while he pointed the fat muzzle of the silenced Sidewinder at the nearest boy. "No, all I brought you is grief. Don't make any noise and do as you're told and you'll get through this alive."

"Who the fuck are you?" the older youth asked with the cracking tone of adolescence.

"Lay down on your bellies, spread eagle. Do it or you get a bullet."

The startled boys hastened to obey. The Penetrator knelt beside the younger guard and secured wrists and ankles with strip-plastic riot cuffs. Then he bound the second lad. That accomplished, he gagged and searched them both. Before he departed he offered them some advice.

"Be glad you're out of it. Someone's going to get hurt tonight and I don't intend for it to be me."

When Mark rendezvoused with Kim they quickly compared results. "They're gettin' better at hiding things," Kim began. "I'd been willing to swear there weren't any guards out. I ran into two of those damn kids in a machine-gun emplacement and another pair yackin' together under a tree."

The Penetrator told him of his own encounter. Then he added an observation based on far too little information.

"Looks like the North Korean troops have been called off for some reason. Maybe to form the lead elements of the invasion force since they know about the kids. Let's get on in there before they change the guard mount."

Confidence didn't betray the Penetrator into suicidal boldness. He moved in short rushes from the deep shadows of one darkened building to another until halfway across the clearing toward a concrete bunker inset into a mountain side. He came up short, reflexes tautly jangling, at the sudden clatter of metal.

The Penetrator took a quick, cautious peek around the corner of the small shed he sheltered behind. A sleepy Korean sergeant, uniform blouse unbuttoned and missing his cap, had kicked a scrub bucket carelessly left at the edge of the drill field. He cursed it and the malefactor who had abandoned it and continued to advance directly toward where the Penetrator stood in hiding.

Without a break in stride, the sergeant rounded the corner, headed toward the distant guard shack. The Penetrator had withdrawn and now swung his Sidewinder into line for a close shot. Too close, it turned out.

The three slugs in the short, chuffing burst went in low, stitching the sergeant across both hips and his groin. He fell to the ground screaming and thrashing in agony.

"What's that noise?" a gruff voice demanded in Korean.

"Who's out there?"

"Corporal of the guard! Corporal of the guard!"

The Penetrator silenced the wailing soldier with a bullet in the head. The damage, unfortunately, had already been done.

Bright lights illuminated the parade ground and Korean soldiers, who had been given the night off now that their work had been completed, came pouring from the guardhouse and their own barracks. Several of them loosed off shots in the direction of their wounded comrade's cries. Then the children dashed out the door of their quarters, half of them armed and firing wild shots in every direction. Over the din, the Penetrator heard Kim's voice calling in an attempt to misdirect the alerted garrison toward the perimeter.

"Over there! Over there! Yankee soldiers!" Kim appeared in the harsh illumination of the drill field, waving one arm toward the brush. He fired a burst from an AK-74 into the innocent trees and charged in that direction. Some of the soldiers followed him.

The Penetrator took advantage of the confusion to change position to the side of another building, nearer, but still on the wrong side of the parade ground from the bunker. He tensed and waited.

Gunfire sounded from beyond the spot where Kim had disappeared. Answering blasts came from several directions. A grenade crumphed and momentarily lighted the forest with a yellow-orange flash. Another racketing burst came from a 5.56mm Kalashnikov and then silence.

Three soldiers came back into the compound. They cast wary glances over their shoulders into the underbrush. For a moment no one else moved. The Penetrator looked from place to place, yet saw no sign of Kim.

# 18

## DEATH OF A PLAN

"Get back to your rooms, boys and girls," a voice boomed over the PA system. "Stop firing and return to your rooms. This is Colonel Gee. Let the troops handle this. Go back to your quarters and remain quiet until daylight."

The Penetrator crouched in darkness and watched the deadly youngsters file back into the barracks building. In less than two minutes, only the Korean soldiers, alert, weapons ready to repell any further attack, patrolled the compound. With Kim gone, the Penetrator knew he could never cross the lighted parade ground without a challenge that would end the game for him. He extended the telescoping stock of his Sidewinder and knelt. He took careful aim at the furthest cluster of brightly glowing globes.

Mark felt the gently rhythmic cycling of the submachine gun's jolt as he sent a buzzing line of .45 slugs toward the target. Glass tinkled and the filaments glowed orange through brief puffs of smoke and broken glass. In an instant the illumination of the field decreased by a third. The Penetrator changed position and loosed off a long burst at the next stanchion.

More lights died and two soldiers rushed toward the Penetrator. Mark cut them down and quickly changed magazines. He swung the Sidewinder in a low arc, expecting more trouble.

An orange flame wavered in the second-story window of the barracks and a stream of 5.56mm jacketed slugs crackled into the weathered clapboads above Mark's head.

The Penetrator dived for the ground, rolled to one side, and came up blasting. His extended burst hosed expanding .45 JHP's along the barracks and into the dark hole of the window. A soldier screamed a brief wail of agony and flopped halfway out, his blood a crimson flood down the side of the building. Mark dashed to better cover behind a low stone structure and turned his attention to the remaining lights, behind and to the right of him.

The Sidewinder uttered a sustained cough and blackness engulfed the area. The Penetrator surged to his feet, intent on reaching the bunker before the enemy troops could recover from the sudden darkness. Running footsteps slapped the hard earth behind him and the Penetrator whirled, panther-quick, his finger tightening on the Sidewinder's trigger until he heard a familiar voice.

"Hey, man, it's me."

"Kim! I thought you bought it out there."

"Naw. But I did manage to get through to the other side by radio. Our people over there are gonna lay on a little surprise for these bastards."

"Such as what?"

"They're gonna walk a little line right though the compound, starting from the far side over there."

To Mark's dubious frown, he went on. "Nothin' simpler. The boys south of the DMZ have had everything over here registered for years. That ought to start one hell of a panic."

As though to emphasize Kim's prediction, the Penetrator heard a feathery rippling through the air far above him. A line of bright, apocalyptically loud explosions mushroomed along the northern edge of the clearing. More of the deadly missiles roared overhead.

"Four-inch mortars, man!" Kim yelled over the din. "That'll bring down scalding pee."

"When those kids break under fire, get to them and lead them toward the DMZ," the Penetrator ordered. "I'm going after Gee."

"Good luck, Greg."

"Thanks, I'll need it. Good luck to you."

Kim disappeared into the blast-illuminated darkness, toward the barracks, and the Penetrator headed in the other direction, across the parade ground. He pushed his way without incident through a cluster of confused, disoriented soldiers and entered the bunker.

Only the soft glow of red battle lights illuminated a low corridor that ran far into the hillside. The Penetrator checked each room that opened off the central hallway, weapon in hand. From outside he heard the nearly continuous dull thumps of detonating mortar rounds as the powerful shells from the South Korean lines continued to do their job of disrupting the camp. At the far end he came to a closed door.

A burst from his Sidewinder shattered the bolt. The Penetrator kicked open the door and flattened himself against the thick concrete wall to one side. To his surprise, no return fire came from the room.

"Colonel Gee? Come on out. The battle's over and you might as well surrender."

"Ah, yes," came a mocking voice from inside. "The man they call the Penetrator if I'm not mistaken. Indeed, who else could it be? DiFalco and Sasson both killed, their camps abandoned and the children disappeared into the bush. Oh, yes, I received a communiqué on that only half an hour ago." Gee chuckled in mirthless derision.

"You know, when David Felder first told me about you, I believed you were a myth. Some sort of folk hero, like that Englishman, Robin Hood, invented to provide the proletariat with a safe outlet for their frustrations. You have no idea how pleased I am to discover that you are real."

"Quit stalling, colonel. Come on out here with your hands up."

"You realize that you are in my country, don't you? How do you propose to get me out for proper punishment? Or are you going to gun me down in cold blood?"

"Five seconds, colonel, then I come in after you."

Again Gee released that icy, derisive laughter. "Come now, Mr. Penetrator. How recklessly heroic of you. I have a submachine gun here. I presume you have one too. We've reached what you Americans call a, ah, Mexican standoff, am I right?"

"I also have a hand grenade," the Penetrator kept his voice flat, determined.

"Spoilsport. All right, I'll come out."

"Throw the gun ahead of you."

To the Penetrator's surprise, a well-cared-for, like-new Smith and Wesson M-76 submachine gun clattered to the concrete floor of the bunker corridor. Following it by a second, came a cheap, Chinese copy of the Colt New Service, .45 revolver. Then Colonel Gee emerged from the room. He walked with swaying, dance-like steps that reminded the Penetrator of the Indonesian fighting style called *pentjak-silat.* Colonel Gee turned with a confident smile on his lips to face the man who had vanquished him.

Suddenly his foot lashed out in a *sepak terajang,* a *pentjak-silat* kicking technique that ripped the Sidewinder from the Penetrator's grasp and sent it crashing against the ceiling. It fell to the floor with enough force to bend the silencer tube. Immediately Gee continued his *peninjuan bersilat* forward spring.

An expert in several of the more esoteric Oriental martial arts, Gee unleashed all his skill in a determined attempt to kill his opponent.

Caught by surprise for an instant, the Penetrator assumed a *T dachi* stance and warded off Gee's first bare-hand *tikam menikam* stabbing technique—which resembled a *yon hon nukite* four-finger spear attack—with a *kakete uke nagashi* hook and sweep block.

Gee continued through his assault, striking simultaneously with one foot and a hand. The Penetrator side-stepped the kick and blocked Gee's whistling hand blow with a *haishu uke* backhand that he turned into a *shuto uchi* chop that mashed the trapezius muscle between Gee's neck and left shoulder, but failed to contact the nerve ganglion. Gee grunted and stepped back.

Once more Gee started the graceful, swaying steps of *pentjak-silat.*

The Penetrator uttered his piercing, paralyzing Cheyenne war cry and launched his own attack. He broke through Gee's defense with a *morote zuki* u-punch and immediately lashed out with a *fumikomi* front stamp kick. Gee's soft, quickly stifled cry of pain blended with the cracking sound of the bones at his knee. Gee sank to the ground, supporting himself on his uninjured leg.

Gee drew a long knife from his belt sheath and slashed at his foe while he employed *elak mengelak* techniques to avoid further attack. The Penetrator moved in, constantly changing positions, to try another kick and felt hot pain rush up his leg when the blade in Gee's hand bit an inch deep into his left thigh. Mark sprang back and concentrated on a new approach.

"You are being used, you know," the Penetrator spoke for the first time since the deadly fight began. "You and all North Korea. The men who control the SIE have no love for you. You're nothing but cannon fodder to advance their own goal of world conquest."

"You speak words like those of the paranoid radical right newspapers," Gee grunted through his pain. "Together Korea and China shall share the Orient. It is destined, the true wave of the future. Therefore, the SIE means nothing to us."

The Penetrator laughed aloud. "Hopeless dreams of dead men. All the SIE wants is to have Koreans bleed while they get richer. Where's the honor in that? Where the victory?"

Gee swung with the knife again, missed by a

fraction of an inch. "Stop your senseless chatter and fight like a man."

The Penetrator sized up the amount of endurance he believed his challenger had left, then moved in.

Instantly Gee thrust straight forward, risking his precarious balance in an attempt to drive the blade into the Penetrator's groin.

The Penetrator stopped the treacherous attack with a *gedan juji uke* downward X block. He quickly countered with a *teisho* palm heel blow under the point of Gee's chin.

The North Korean colonel's head slammed backward and the Penetrator followed through with a *yubi basami* knuckle-fingertip strike that crushed Gee's throat an inch above the larynx.

Gee emitted a gargling sound, chest pumping to gain the desperately needed air that his destroyed windpipe would not convey. His face purpled and his eyes bulged. He fell onto one side and offered up a weak, childlike groan, then went slackly into death.

The Penetrator gathered up his weapons and entered Gee's office. He destroyed the final file on the children and staggered toward the entrance to the bunker.

"You must be Mr. Miller," a smiling, genial man in the uniform and insignia of a South Korean army colonel greeted a weary Mark Hardin when he arrived at the command-post tent a quarter mile below the DMZ.

"Yes—I am."

"Good, good. Take a chair. The children are reported crossing the DMZ in safe order. At first we couldn't believe it. Two small boys appeared here last night, Robbie and Petey they called themselves. They told the strangest tale. Then we received communication from Captain Ree. You know the rest from there. Well . . ." The colonel poured coffee into a canteen cup, handed it to the Penetrator.

"So far no warlike rumbles from the northern scum. Unfortunately, Captain Ree received a serious wound. He was treated here and taken to Seoul by med-evac chopper."

The Penetrator raised an eyebrow. "*Captain Ree?*"

"Yes, of course. Kim Suŏng Ree. But I thought you knew. I supposed he was a colleague of yours. He's from our own Korean CIA."

"I'm not with the Company."

"Oh?"

"Colonel, I'm tired, I've got some minor wounds that need looking at and I haven't time to explain. What I need most is access to a telephone. Not a field rig, something I can make a call to the States on"

"I—ah, I'll see to it right away."

Ten minutes later, the Penetrator spoke to Dan Griggs.

"It's all over, Dan. The kids are coming in here in bunches and will be held by the Korean authorities until transfer back to the States."

"The gentlemen in charge?"

"Terminated. All records destroyed. This isn't over yet, Dan. Something has to be done to stop the invasion force from crossing the line."

"I'm to see the president in an hour. Perhaps he

and his advisors will have worked out something."

"You haven't got more than two days."

"Nothing has changed here. If we move at all, it will be nothing short of miraculous. And you will never be able to say a word about Felder or the SIE or anything. Too many big friends in high places in government and business. Damnit, they're untouchable."

"That's what Capone and the boys in Chicago thought before Elliot Ness moved in on them."

"Hey! Now, look, fella. None of that stuff. You hear me?"

"Good-bye, Dan." The Penetrator forced down a yawn as he put up the receiver. The strain of the past seventy-two hours had caught up with him.

Tommy Yamato met the Penetrator at Haneda Airport when he returned from Seoul. The young employee of Toro Baldwin greeted Mark effusively and steered him to a waiting limousine. At the Tokyo Hilton a suite waited. Mark went up, still making protests to Tommy, and entered.

Angie Dillon stood in the middle of the room.

"What—Angie—I—"

"A little present from the boss. Toro thought you two would enjoy a little reunion." Tommy produced an ice bucket with a bottle of Dom Perignon '73 to reveal the rest of Baldwin's present.

The Penetrator made no answer. He was too busy kissing Angie.

Much later, after Mark had showered and they had made long, magical love, he and Angie sat in the living room of the suite Toro Baldwin had arranged. On the television set, a Japanese commentator was telling viewers about the American president's announcement that joint Korean-U.S. exercises were to be held over the next two weeks. Ten thousand fresh American troops would be arriving in Seoul, to add to security forces near the DMZ. The unscheduled maneuvers were a part of what the president called "Operation Preparedness."

Even had Mark and Angie been able to understand the Japanese commentary, they would have paid scant attention.

They had each other.

A spectacular new fantasy adventure series from America's #1 series publisher!

## ROSS ANTON COE

# WARRIOR OF VENGEANCE

#1

## SORCERER'S BLOOD

In the epic sword and sorcery
tradition of the mighty Conan, here
is the blood-laden new
adventure series about a pre-medieval
warrior who confronts wild boars,
monstrous eelsharks, man-eating centipedes,
mind-controlled zombies, murderous
raiders, vengeful allies... and the
greatest wizard of them all — Talmon Khash.

# Best-Selling Sports Books
# from Pinnacle